L3.

200 HARLEY STREET

Welcome to the luxurious premises of
the exclusive Hunter Clinic, world renowned
in plastic and reconstructive surgery,
set right on Harley Street, the centre of
elite clinical excellence, in the heart of
London's glittering West End!

Owned by two very different brothers,
Leo and Ethan Hunter, the Hunter Clinic
undertakes both cosmetic and reconstructive
surgery. Playboy Leo handles the rich and
famous clients, enjoying the red carpet
glamour of London's A-list social scene,
while brooding ex-army doc Ethan
focuses his time on his passion—
transforming the lives of injured war heroes
and civilian casualties of war.

Emotion and drama abound against the
backdrop of one of Europe's most glamorous
cities, as Leo and Ethan work
through their tensions and find women
who will change their lives for ever!

200 HARLEY STREET

*Glamour, intensity, desire—the lives and loves
of London's hottest team of surgeons!*

Dear Reader

It's always exciting to be a part of a big continuity and I was fortunate to be asked to participate in this one along with seven other authors. The combination worked a bit like a recipe: Take one group of breath-taking characters in a chic plastic surgery clinic setting, add eight enthusiastic writers, mix well with fabulous storylines from the editors, bake slowly to seal in the passion, serve warm with a dollop of wonderful. The name of this creation? **200 Harley Street**.

I get to tell Mitchell and Grace's story in book number four. Grace is running away from her life in Arizona, taking a job in London as a reconstructive surgeon. This is a profession near and dear to her heart, as she can relate to her patients on more levels than meets the eye. Mitchell is also American, and has been living and working in London for a few years already. He is a plastic surgeon at the Hunter Clinic as well as the doting father of young daughter, Mia, and he will do anything to make the young one's life stable. Mitch doesn't realise that, on the night he takes over host duties at a charity benefit held at the London Eye, his and Mia's lives will change forever.

Have you ever met someone and never intended to get to know them, but immediately hit it off, and end up hanging out together for one evening? Neither have I, LOL, that's why I enjoyed writing Mitchell and Grace's story. I got to throw these two wounded characters together on one special night, let them forget their troubles and develop a harmless crush in a safe setting, then pull them apart leaving them both with a deep yearning for something more in their lives.

Next stop the Hunter Clinic where the cast of characters is fun and entertaining, even though each character has a difficult story to tell. Now it's got to be all business between Mitchell and Grace. There's just one problem, their attraction to each other is too strong to ignore, and resist as they may these two future lovebirds cannot keep apart. Add little Mia into the mix and whether they realise it at first or not, they've completed their perfect little circle of three.

File this story under—a readymade family meant to be together.

I love to hear from my readers. You can contact me at my website: www.lynnemarshall.com and friend me on Facebook!

Wishing you happy reading,

Lynne

200 HARLEY STREET: AMERICAN SURGEON IN LONDON

BY
LYNNE MARSHALL

First published in Great Britain 2014
by Mills & Boon, an imprint of Harlequin (UK) Limited,
Large Print edition 2014
Eton House, 18-24 Paradise Road,
Richmond, Surrey, TW9 1SR

© 2014 Harlequin Books S.A.

Special thanks and acknowledgement are given to Lynne Marshall for her contribution to the *200 Harley Street* series

ISBN: 978-0-263-23909-6

Printed and bound in Great Britain
by CPI Antony Rowe, Chippenham, Wiltshire

Dedication

For my husband of thirty-one years. I'm so glad I found you.
And special thanks to Flo for inviting me into this continuity.

Lynne Marshall used to worry she had a serious problem
with daydreaming—then she discovered she was supposed
to write those stories down! A late bloomer, Lynne came
to fiction-writing after being a registered nurse for twenty-
five years and when her children were nearly grown. Now
she battles the empty nest by writing stories from her heart,
which always include a romance with a touch of medicine
for both Medical Romance™ and Special Edition. She is a
Southern California native, a woman of faith, a dog-lover,
and a curious traveller.

To find out more about Lynne, please visit her website:
www.lynnemarshall.com

Recent titles by Lynne Marshall:

NYC ANGELS: MAKING THE SURGEON SMILE*
DR TALL, DARK…AND DANGEROUS?
THE CHRISTMAS BABY BUMP
THE HEART DOCTOR AND THE BABY
THE BOSS AND NURSE ALBRIGHT
TEMPORARY DOCTOR, SURPRISE FATHER

NYC Angels

**These books are also available in eBook format
from www.millsandboon.co.uk**

Praise for Lynne Marshall:

'Heartfelt emotion that will bring you to the point of tears,
for those who love a second-chance romance
written with exquisite detail.'
—*Contemporary Romance Reviews* on
NYC ANGELS: MAKING THE SURGEON SMILE

'Lynne Marshall contributes a rewarding story
to the *NYC Angels* series, and her gifted talent repeatedly
shines. MAKING THE SURGEON SMILE is an outstanding
romance with genuine emotions and passionate desires.'
—*Cataromance* on
NYC ANGELS: MAKING THE SURGEON SMILE

200 HARLEY STREET

*Glamour, intensity, desire—the lives and loves of
London's hottest team of surgeons!*

**For the next four months enter the world of London's
elite surgeons as they transform the lives of their patients
and find love amidst a sea of passions and tensions…!**

Renowned plastic surgeon and legendary playboy
Leo Hunter can't resist the challenge of unbuttoning
the intriguing new head nurse, Lizzie Birch!
200 HARLEY STREET: SURGEON IN A TUX
by Carol Marinelli

Glamorous Head of PR Lexi Robbins is determined
to make gruff, grieving and super-sexy Scottish surgeon Iain MacKenzie
her Hunter Clinic star!
200 HARLEY STREET: GIRL FROM THE RED CARPET
by Scarlet Wilson

Top-notch surgeons and estranged spouses
Rafael and Abbie de Luca find being forced to work together again
tough as their passion is as incendiary as ever!
200 HARLEY STREET: THE PROUD ITALIAN
by Alison Roberts

One night with his new colleague, surgeon Grace Turner, sees
former Hollywood plastic surgeon Mitchell Cooper daring to live again…
200 HARLEY STREET: AMERICAN SURGEON IN LONDON
by Lynne Marshall

Injured war hero Prince Marco meets physical therapist
Becca Anderson—the woman he once shared a magical *forbidden*
summer romance with long ago…
200 HARLEY STREET: THE SOLDIER PRINCE
by Kate Hardy

When genius micro-surgeon Edward North meets single mum
Nurse Charlotte King she opens his eyes to a whole new world…
200 HARLEY STREET: THE ENIGMATIC SURGEON
by Annie Claydon

Junior surgeon Kara must work with hot-shot
Irish surgeon Declan Underwood—the man she kissed at the hospital ball!
200 HARLEY STREET: THE SHAMELESS MAVERICK
by Louisa George

Brilliant charity surgeon Olivia Fairchild faces the man who once
broke her heart—damaged ex-soldier Ethan Hunter. Yet she's unprepared
for his haunted eyes and the shock of his sensual touch…!
200 HARLEY STREET: THE TORTURED HERO by Amy Andrews

**Experience glamour, tension, heartbreak and emotion
at 200 HARLEY STREET
in this new eight-book continuity
from Mills & Boon® Medical Romance™**

**These books are also available in eBook format
and in two 200 HARLEY STREET collection bundles
from www.millsandboon.co.uk**

CHAPTER ONE

GRACE TURNER GLANCED around the perfectly appointed guest apartment—cream-colored walls, beige couch and a matching club chair, with half a dozen colorful pillows strategically placed, red accent chair on the opposite side, fresh-cut white calla lilies in a tall vase on the glass-topped coffee table. There was even a small cherrywood desk pushed into the corner with internet hookup. Her laptop fit perfectly there.

Everything was in place for her convenience, and she was definitely thankful to the Hunter Clinic for the comfort in her new home away from home. The apartment was also supposed to be a mere ten-minute walk around the corner to 200 Harley Street and her new job.

Her gaze drifted into the single bedroom with the extra-large bed. *That's not going to see any action. A single wide would have been more than adequate*. Surrounded by luxury and taste to the hilt, the guest apartment was already closing in on her and she needed to get out. Desperately.

The extended-stay hotel was fully serviced, and though she hadn't had a chance to shop for food yet, she didn't feel like ordering room service. She'd heard of a tiny car-free street somewhere nearby, also within walking distance, where she could window-shop and dine alfresco, but she was sick of being alone. And why bother to buy new clothes when she didn't have anyone to wear them for?

She paced the length of the living room, noticed the invitation placed carefully on her mantelpiece before her arrival from the States yesterday, and picked it up. It was a duplicate of the one sent to her a couple of months back. Frankly, she'd forgotten all about the fundraising event at the London Eye tonight. Leo Hunter, the man who'd personally asked her to join his clinic, had said he'd be attending. The combination of meeting her new boss a day early and in a more casual setting at a charity event, and a bit of fun on the

London Eye sounded like the perfect antidote for her early-onset cabin fever.

Grace strode to the eye-popping white kitchen and put on some water for tea. Even though she was tired, she felt too restless to sleep. She needed a little caffeine to ward off the quickly approaching fatigue from the long flight. Then she headed for the bedroom to find the perfect outfit.

Never an easy chore, finding fashionable clothes that covered her scars, Grace burrowed through her two suitcases, tossing tops, dresses, slacks, and underwear every which way. Making a mental note to put things in the drawers and closet at her earliest convenience, she continued to dig through the luggage. Ah, there was the black lace bodysuit, the one with a mock turtle-neck and wrist-length sleeves. It would go perfectly under that low-cut black evening dress with the puffy shoulders and cap sleeves, and the above the knee-length dress would showcase her best attribute—her legs.

It being May in London, she could definitely get away with bundling up for the clear but chilly evening. No one would raise an eyebrow about the extra layer of underclothing, especially as it was sexy. She'd discovered over the years that there was nothing quite like fine black lace to cover up the scars.

An hour later, invitation in hand, a new layer of makeup carefully applied, and with a glittery fake jeweled barrette in her hair just for fun, she made her way toward the apartment door.

Grace felt like a kid again. Getting out of the taxi near Westminster Bridge, her eyes went to the huge, brightly lit, famous Ferris wheel. The cabbie instructed her toward the entrance, and off she went, entranced by the huge ride, following the spectacle that filled up this part of the London skyline. Showing her invitation to the official-looking security guard, she was let inside the gate. A fairly large crowd of impeccably dressed people of all shapes and ages milled around, chatting, sipping drinks and eating tidbits provided by tuxedo-dressed helpers with flashy silver trays.

Though she was considered wealthy back home by Scottsdale, Arizona standards, they paled in comparison with tonight's larger-than-life festivities. She ate a salmon puff, sipped some champagne and looked for a familiar face. The only face she knew, actually, and that was from an interview on world-renowned plastic surgery clinics she'd seen on TV, was Leo Hunter's.

A half hour later, still circulating through the crowd, a gaze here, a nod there, a smile every once in a while, she noticed one particularly grandly dressed couple get off the Eye. She'd seen them get on—she checked her watch—about half an hour ago. Still unsuccessful in finding Leo Hunter, she decided to quit looking for him and take the ride.

She might not be able to meet Leo tonight, but she could at least grab a few quiet moments and take in the amazing sights of London all lit up. She read a sign with a few facts about the Eye. After doing some quick mental math, converting meters to feet, she took a deep breath, realizing she'd soon be more than four hundred feet in the air. Her phobia wasn't fear of heights so much as fear of falling. She glanced at the sturdy-looking steel-and-glass pods, convincing herself they'd hold. But she'd keep safely away from the windows. So she walked up the ramp and, with the Eye closed to the public for the charity event, was able to follow a handful of people onto the next pod.

One man already on board didn't bother to get off.

Two middle-aged couples talked quietly on one side of the egg-shaped pod. She nodded at them and they smiled, but clearly their circle of friends was closed to outsiders. She considered sitting on the wooden bench in the middle to help lessen her fear of falling, but changed her mind.

On the other side of the pod, that single figure taking a second trip gazed outside. Something about him drew her to his side of the pod. From behind, he had broad shoulders that filled out his tuxedo perfectly, and rich brown hair that kissed the collar on his shirt. He seemed closer to her age than the others, too. He leaned against the rail, shoulder to the glass, arms folded, deep in thought. She took a tentative step closer, not invading his privacy but close enough to see his profile.

Wow. The man was nothing short of gorgeous, with a high forehead, strong brows and jaw, a nose that could be claimed perfect if it wasn't for the attractive bump on the bridge. The decisive cleft in his chin was almost overkill. Speaking strictly as a reconstructive surgeon, this guy was a natural work of art. Even the shell of his ear was attractive.

She'd never been one to swoon over looks, especially in her line of work, when she knew people could alter their appearances to be more perfect looking, but this man in all his glory elicited chill bumps. Tingles danced along the skin of her arms and up the back of her neck as he awakened something inside her, long forgotten.

She took in a slow breath to steady herself. Perhaps it was the fact the pod had reached a point where she realized she'd soon be dangling from a height almost twice that of the Statue of Liberty that made her knees weaken. She snuck another glance at him and reached for the rail.

There was something more than pure handsomeness in this man. Something about his brooding, the tight upper lip and mildly pouting lower lip, how lost in his thoughts he seemed. There was something about his dissatisfaction about God only knew what that drew her in. Unfortunately, she'd always been a sucker for brooders. And she was definitely drawn to his contemplation, against her will maybe, but will seemed to have nothing to do with it. She couldn't stop herself from staring.

He was a perfectly made man who, from the expression on his face, seemed perfectly miserable, and that was the part that touched her most—it made him someone she could relate to.

"Hi," she said to him, surprising herself, but what the hell, if she was going to spend the next half hour dangling above the Thames, she may as well be talking to the handsomest man she'd ever laid her eyes on. Who knew? Regardless of the millions of people who'd already ridden it safely, something could go wrong on the Eye tonight. For all she knew, this might be the last thirty minutes of her life.

Wouldn't it be smart to spend those last minutes staring into the most intense eyes she'd ever seen?

Grace smiled to herself, thinking she'd officially turned into a fatalistic drama queen. Apparently the handsome stranger's doom and gloom had rubbed off on her.

This was the last place Mitch Cooper wanted to be tonight, but Leo had needed someone to cover for him while he and Lizzie were seeing a travel agent about their upcoming honeymoon in Paris. Between Leo and this highly sought-after travel agent's schedules, the appointment landed at eight o'clock on a Sunday night.

The black-tie affair had been on the calendar long before Leo had finally seen the light and popped the question to the head nurse at the Hunter Clinic. Though the newly marrieds had put off their honeymoon until the summer, he understood the guy needed an extra night off duty every now and again.

Mitch would rather be home, reading a goodnight book to Mia. Sure, Roberta was there, but no nanny could replace a father's love—or a mother's.

He braced himself for more nights like these,

since Leo had asked his surgeons to step in and help with the multiple and necessary social functions and fund-raisers related to the Hunter Clinic. Especially now that Leo had gotten married, he'd want a life away from the clinic and that meant the rest of them attending more events. And as a team player, Mitch would do his share.

After all, the clinic with the wealthy donors who kept things running for the sake of those in need, not to mention the eternally nipping-and-tucking plastics patients, was everyone's bread and butter. If he wanted to stake out a new life for himself in London, and provide the kind of life he dreamed of for his daughter, this small price to pay wasn't so bad.

Tonight he'd rubbed elbows with as many guests as humanly possible. He'd made the rounds, done his duty and had now decided to sneak off and take in the view one more time before heading home. He'd have to bring Mia here one day. She'd love it.

He really did love London, especially after dark, and most especially after leaving Hollywood and all the bad memories behind.

Someone spoke—a woman. He dragged himself out of his dark thoughts, which always managed at quiet times like these to circle back to his ex-wife and best friend.

"Hi," he said robotically, looking straight ahead. "Enjoying yourself?" Then, back on duty and clicking into host mode, he actually glanced at the person to his left.

Time slowed as he took in the strikingly beautiful woman. Large and inquisitive pale eyes, enhanced by dark eyeliner and curtained by thick bangs, stared expectantly at him. Having never seen her before, because he'd definitely remember this face if he had, he assumed she was a wealthy donor.

With no sign of plastic surgery or Botox injections, she smiled naturally, with fine crinkles beside her eyes and mouth. Her cheeks grew more prominent, and that sweet little mouth with meticulously applied pink lipstick stretched into a serene smile. The sight of such a lovely face buoyed his spirits nearly to the height of the pod.

Could he be so superficial, letting natural beauty grab him like this? Yes, and his broken marriage proved it. Hadn't he learned his lesson? "Have you been to the London Eye before?"

She shook her head of dark hair—half of it piled high on her crown and with a shiny barrette meant for nothing more than show, something his daughter might wear—the rest of the hair dropping in waves around her neck. "I'm new in town."

Probably here for some plastic-surgery work since tonight's guests were by invitation only. All the beautiful women he'd ever known thought of plastic surgery as their little beauty secret. Maybe he could talk her out of whatever procedure she'd come to have. Why mess with genuine perfection? God, he hoped she didn't plan to change her lips. They were just fine as they were, with the classically shaped Cupid's-bow upper lip and the plump lower mate. Bigger was not always better, and lip jobs never looked completely natural, in his opinion. Even under his skilled hands.

"If you're new in town, then I guess I need to be a gentleman and point out a few landmarks, don't I?"

She continued to smile and her expression

changed to one of playfulness. "Definitely. By the way, I notice you're American, too."

He nodded. "I'm from California originally. How about you?"

"Arizona."

Didn't they have highly acclaimed plastic surgery clinics in Scottsdale? Maybe, as Scottsdale could be a tight-knit small town, she didn't want anyone to know she was undergoing a procedure. Maybe she'd told everyone she was going on vacation, and when she went home she'd look amazingly well rested. Who knew? Who cared? Maybe he should quit reading so many sleuth novels and stop assuming the worst about women.

Right now, he'd grab a moment for himself and enjoy it with…what was her name?

"I'm Mitchell, by the way, and you are?"

"Grace. Nice to meet you."

Yes, of course her name would be Grace, she almost shimmered with it.

"So, Grace, across the Thames there you'll notice Big Ben, and the Gothic-style building with all of those lights right on the river are the Houses of Parliament."

She followed wherever he pointed, smiled and nodded. He liked it that she'd stepped a little closer and a refreshing, brisk, fruity scent floated up his nose. She wore a sexy black dress with a diving neckline, but instead of flaunting everything God had given her—there he went assuming again, but her breasts were probably real as they were shapely but not overly large—she'd covered up with amazingly alluring thin black lace. Sexy. And not fair. The subtle holding back made him all the more curious about what lay beneath. Some women knew how to make a man take notice and beg for more. Hats off to the beautiful Grace from Arizona.

He cleared his throat, forcing his thoughts back on task. "Oh, and over there is Westminster Abbey. Look down just a bit more. There."

She inched forward and grimaced when she glanced downward.

"Fear of heights?"

"Fear of falling."

"Ah. I promise I won't push you or swing the pod." She smiled and another moment stopped in time. He grasped for something to say.

"Remember trying to make the Ferris-wheel gondolas swing when you were a kid?"

She gave him an incredulous and funny look.

He grinned. "Maybe that was just a guy thing. Anyway, I'll point out a few more places...."

She oohed and ahhed over everything, giving him the impression he was doing a fantastic job as a tour guide. Maybe he could start a second career? But then again, maybe she was easily pleased.

"The lights make everything so much more beautiful, don't they?" she said, her sweet, husky voice soothing every wrinkle in his mind.

The sparkling city lights reflected off the pod window and dappled her face in shimmering whites and muted colors. He dipped his head in agreement with her statement—the lights did make everything look more beautiful, especially her.

They continued the rest of the ride in casual conversation, just two Americans in London sharing a fun moment together. It was a hell of a lot better than what he'd been doing before she'd spoken to him.

She laughed easily when he tried to be charming and he liked that—made him want to keep talking. He also liked it that her fashionable shoes made her only a couple of inches shy of his six feet—all the better to stare into those amazingly vibrant blue eyes.

Suddenly energized, as the pod ended its full circle journey, and not wanting to say goodbye to the lovely lady, he got a crazy idea. Ask her out. Why not?

But he was so out of practice at spending time with women. Didn't have a clue what she might like to do. Where did the only female that mattered in his life like to go best? "Do you enjoy swinging?"

A shocked and offended expression replaced Grace's prior childlike enjoyment. She really had a way with giving "looks" that said it all.

Realizing his unintentional allusion to carefree sex—*swinging*—he raced to make things right. "On swings, I mean. Actual swings. Uh, the kind you sit on. Swinging?"

She blurted out a laugh, relief softening her

eyes. "Oh. Well, in that case...I haven't been on a swing in ages."

The pod door opened. The other couples exited. He took her by the arm and led her out. "I know a place nearby—that is, if you're up for it. We could walk over. Maybe have a drink afterwards?" He let go of her arm, not wanting to seem overbearing. "No strings." He gazed earnestly into her blue—yes, they were definitely blue—eyes. "What do you say?"

He'd laid it on the line, stuck out his neck and set himself up to be humiliated with a firm no, but he couldn't help it. Something about her had made him ask. Suddenly, his only desire was to spend more time with this woman.

But for all she knew, he could be a London serial killer. He, on the other hand, had known immediately that she definitely wasn't a serial killer, just a lovely lady biding her time before "donating" to the Hunter Clinic.

"I'm still on Arizona time, everything's all mixed up, but I'm not ready to turn in yet. Sure. Why not?"

Apparently as good at reading people as he

was, she, and their mutual trust of strangers at charity events, overcame all her doubts. And he couldn't have been happier with her decision.

The man named Mitch—and she was perfectly happy not knowing his full name, because once she began her new job she wouldn't have a spare moment to get to know anyone outside work any-way—grabbed each of them some champagne in a plastic flute and directed her out of the gate. Facing away from the Thames, they turned left and soon came upon a few straggling street art-ists, no doubt holding out for the last of the tour-ists of the day. Or night. She checked her watch, it was almost ten.

One street artist was completely silver and stood on a small box with a large jar for tips at his feet. His head was shaved, he wore a suit and was reading a book. Perfectly still. Another fellow wore a fedora and a raincoat, all bronze from head to toe, arms folded, one foot forward looking like something from out of the forties or fifties.

"What if their nose itches?" she said, taking a long sip of her bubbly, admiring the live art.

Mitch laughed. "I'll ask." He stepped forward, dug into his pocket and put a bill into the tip jar. "What do you do if your nose itches?"

The pavement artist slowly and believably came to life. First his eyes moved, then he twitched his nose. He unfolded his arms and robotically took his index finger and ran it up and down the bridge of his nose. Then, just as methodically, as if he were a machine or wind-up toy, he returned to his original stance.

Grace clapped. "Love it."

Mitch gave her an odd look as he took the crook of her elbow and pulled her down the path. She followed willingly. Halfway down the wide walkway they came upon a huge fenced-off playground on the right.

"This is, bar none, my favorite playground," he said.

Why would he have a favorite playground? Was he married with children? Could her innocent desire to forget and enjoy the night damage someone else's relationship? She slowed. He noticed her hesitation, raising an eyebrow over it.

"I'm just a big kid, I guess."

He said it so matter-of-factly that she didn't pursue the rest of the story. He'd told her everything she needed to know. He was a big kid who happened to know about children's playgrounds.

Yeah, he was probably a dad. A single dad? One could only hope.

But tonight wasn't about making a new friend, learning about family trees, personal baggage, regrets, or joys. Tonight was about letting go and having a little adventure with a complete, and totally handsome, stranger. The less she knew the better. Just to be on the safe side, though, she'd memorized the walk back to the Eye and could get herself there in a flash.

She nodded. He took the cue and they walked to the entrance of the Jubilee Playground, which had a large green sign on the gate.

"'Young adventurers this way,'" he read, glanced at her and winked. "That would be us."

Grace saw the shoulder-high fence railings and closed gate and wondered how they'd manage to get inside, just as two hands took her by the waist and hoisted her upward. He lifted her as if she weighed nothing. "You want to go first? Or should I?"

She suppressed her need to squeal, sucking in a breath instead. "Let me take off my shoes at least."

He put her down and moved a few feet over to an embankment where the fence was much lower. He jumped up on the cement ledge and offered down his hand. She threw her shoes onto the grass and climbed up with his help. To hell with the sexy dress, and thank God she had on the body suit!

His eyes sparkled when he glanced at her just before he jumped the fence. How the hell was she supposed to do that? Realizing his mistake, he jumped back over and helped her up, giving her time to get her footing and gain confidence, and soon, with the help of his cupped hands for her foot, she'd also scaled the fence.

Everything in the playground was made of sturdy logs and wood, encouraging the "young adventurers" to climb and play. Like a man who'd been here a number of times, Mitch led her to the swings and helped her on, then gave her a big push.

He had to be a father. And husband? Oh, no, she hoped not.

She curved into the night, feeling like a kid again. Soon he joined her on another swing and they quietly went about the business of letting down their hair in the cool evening breeze.

"This is great," she said, having pumped her feet enough to take her to the hilt on the swing. "Haven't done this since I don't know when."

"Then I'd say you're overdue. Hey, for someone with a fear of heights, you're awfully high."

"That's 'cause I'm in control."

"Ah, a lady who likes to be in control. How refreshing."

She'd play along with his teasing jab about pushy women. "Watch it, buddy." With that she jumped out of her swing in midair, feeling daring, and more like a kid trying to impress an older boy than a thirty-two-year-old reconstructive surgeon.

He applauded then used his feet to stop his

swing the old-fashioned way. "Want to go down the slide?" He looked directly at her in the darkness of the playground, daring her to take his challenge.

She sputtered a laugh. "In this dress?"

"You climbed the fence and dove out of the swing, didn't you?"

"True," she said, dusting off her hands. "But I really don't want to ruin my dress on a slide." She ignored his dare and walked farther on. "You're probably renting that tuxedo, and don't care what happens to it," she said, one last attempt to save face.

"How about the monkey bars, then?"

"Who's there?" came a gruff voice from over the fence. A high-beamed flashlight danced around the vicinity of the swings. She fought the urge to hide sideways behind a pole. "No trespassing."

"We were just leaving, Officer." Mitch stepped up and offered a hand to Grace. Her heart pounded from the swinging, and now for getting into trouble for it.

She grinned to make up for her nerves and decided to go the teasing route. "That's what I get for going off with a strange man on an adventure. Next I'll be thrown in jail and I've barely been in town twenty-four hours."

The security officer noticed the fact that Mitch wore a tuxedo and she was in an evening dress, and he beetled his brows and tugged his earlobe. "You're not dressed for the playground, are you?"

"No, sir, we're escapees from the Hunter Clinic charity function at London Eye tonight," Mitch said.

The man's expression brightened. "The Hunter Clinic helped my niece when she'd burned her face on a campfire. Wonderful place, that clinic on Harley Street. Now if you'll just run along, I'll let you off with a stern warning."

"Thank you!" Grace called out, walking briskly toward the exit.

The officer stood by and watched with one brow raised as they jumped back over the fence, Mitch helping Grace up and over. Then Mitch shook the man's hand and the officer bid them good-night. They all walked away, the officer one direction, they in another.

"I'm starving. How about you?" Mitch asked, grinning like a kid who'd just gotten away with mischief.

Besides the salmon puff she really hadn't eaten anything today, not yet having had time to stock food in her new kitchen. "Come to think of it, I am, too."

"I know a great place about ten minutes away. You okay to walk in those shoes?" He nodded toward the shoes dangling from her fingers.

"I made it here, didn't I?" She brushed off her skirt with the palm of her free hand and worried about how messed up her hair must look.

He smiled and his white teeth gleamed in the night. It wasn't fair he was that gorgeous. "That's the spirit."

Fifteen minutes later they wound up past the Hungerford Bridge on the third floor of the Royal Festival Hall in an upscale restaurant overlooking the South Bank. They sat at the huge modern wraparound bar with a distinct 1950s-influenced design. The view was gorgeous, and Grace ordered a Cabernet Sauvignon and gnocchi. Mitch ordered a mixed drink and steak.

Up close, in the brighter-than-average lit bar, his eyes were green, more sea-green blue, and she realized she'd gotten lost gazing into them. He must have noticed and lifted the corner of his mouth in an angled smile.

"For someone from the sunny state of Arizona, you have a really creamy complexion," he said.

"I own stock in sunscreen." Feeling flattered he'd noticed something about her, she smiled.

He smiled back, and added a light laugh. Maybe she hadn't lost her touch with social conversation after all, or he was going out of his way to be polite.

It was easy to make him chuckle, and their evening went on in free-flowing banter. No topic scratched below the surface. Somehow they'd made a pact not to really get to know each other. Yet she picked things up, like the fact he hated onions and separated them out of his dinner salad, and even after cavorting in the park he smelled fresh and trendy. The scent probably cost an arm and leg from some designer store. He owned his own tux and he knew where to take children to play.

The nagging question returned. Did he have a wife and family? And if so, who looked after them while he gallivanted around at charity events with strange women? Maybe he was one of the wealthy Hunter donors and could afford to live a double life.

She really needed to quit trying to figure him out and just enjoy his company. After tonight she'd never see him again anyway.

Her gnocchi was delicious and she forced herself to eat slowly. The cabernet warmed her brain and for her first night in London she had to admit she would never have come up with this scenario in her wildest dreams. *Thank you, Leo, for inviting me to the Eye.*

By half past midnight, rather than get to know each other, they'd discussed half a dozen couples from the bar, sizing them up and guessing their circumstances. Then, after making up far-fetched stories about secret agents and international spies along with who the couples must be, they pondered what other people might surmise about them.

"Maybe they think we're two famous doctors

out to save the world," Mitch said, hitting very close to home in Grace's situation.

"How about a rich American actress and her best friend's husband," said Grace, raising her brows, wanting to throw him off track. She must have done a good job as his expression faltered for a millisecond. Oh, no, she'd pushed the game too far. Had she hit a nerve?

The next few moments ticked by in silence, and he seemed to have lost interest in playing the game.

Mitch finished his drink and looked at his watch. "I should get you home."

Okay, she'd definitely hit a nerve, and now she'd ruined their evening. "Yes," she said, suddenly feeling awkward for the first time that night. "I imagine you've got to get home, too." *To your wife and family.*

"I'm divorced, in case you're wondering." His mood had shifted toward all business and she suspected it was because of what she'd hinted at. Or could he read her mind?

He reached for his wallet when the bill came.

"Let me pay for mine, okay?"

He scowled at her, but quickly turned the look playful. "Not on your life. I almost got you into trouble back there. It's the least I can do."

She glanced at the huge run in her hose. "True. And I've ruined my stockings."

"Sorry about that. Maybe I should buy you another drink?"

"No, thanks." She sat straighter. "It was fun. Well worth the cost of new stockings."

"It was, wasn't it?" He left the right amount of cash plus a generous tip and got off the barstool. "We're pod people," he said, offering his hand. "Pod people and young adventurers, and we must stick together."

And total strangers, don't forget.

Grace grinned and accepted his hand to help her down then followed Mitch out of the bar. They took the elevator, more subdued than earlier, though he made eye contact with her several different times. She wondered if he'd ask for her phone number, but he didn't. When they hit the street, he hailed a cab, opened the door and helped her to get in.

"Look," he said, sticking his head inside but

not getting into the taxi, "I've had a great time tonight. You're a beautiful woman, and I thank you for spending these past few hours with me." He sucked in a breath and Grace waited for the "but".

"But I have a demanding job and what extra time I have...well...I don't have time to date." He glanced into her eyes, as if looking for understanding. She held his gaze, not saying a word. She wasn't his type, or... Was this how men who were involved handled things? "If it was a different time in my life. If circumstances were different. The thing is, I just don't have...well...it just wouldn't be fair."

"Shh," she stopped him. She'd heard enough.

He'd made his point quite clear. There was no room for anyone else in his life. He was probably living with someone and had needed a night to himself, that was all. He was an honorable guy who didn't fool around on the side, just hung out with strange ladies.

He'd been the one to say no strings immediately after inviting her to walk with him. What had she expected?

Silly thoughts invaded her mind but nothing could stop the disappointment that came crashing down around her. Though in her heart she knew exactly what he'd meant about not having any time beyond work. Hell, she'd been thinking those very thoughts earlier. She was in London to start a new job as a reconstructive surgeon at the Hunter Clinic on Harley Street, she planned to put her heart and soul into her job, and where did that leave her? Exactly in Mitch's shoes.

There was simply not enough time to have a well-balanced life in her line of work.

Grace reached for his hand and squeezed it. "Thank you so much for this superspecial introduction to London. Every time I look at that overgrown Ferris wheel I'll think of my adventurous pod man and smile."

He grinned, moved in closer and pecked her cheek. "Thank you for understanding."

She lowered her eyelids and nodded. "More than you know."

He connected with her eyes once more; there was that pang of remorse again as they shared a silent agreement—this had only been for tonight.

The poignant moment stretched on until the cabbie cleared his throat.

From the mood she'd slipped into, she'd probably only projected what she thought had been a look of regret in his eyes. She knew for a fact he could detect it in her gaze.

Soon the door shut, he gave the cabbie some money and instructions. "Take the lovely lady home."

As the car pulled away from the curb, and Mitch's scent lingered on, Grace looked out the back window at the most amazing man she'd ever met. He stood there, posed with one hand in his pocket and his head cocked slightly to the side, as if he was a suave street artist, watching her leave.

Whatever or whoever he was, he would forever be etched in her mind as her pod man—quite possibly a figment of her imagination.

But then she glanced down at her legs and saw the gaping rip in her stockings.

No. Adventurous pod man was real. She sighed.

Life sure had a sucky way of rubbing bad timing into her scarred skin, and reminding her she was completely alone and without prospects beyond her new job.

CHAPTER TWO

GRACE WALKED UP the four steps to the classic white building on Harley Street. The twin black doors on either side of a window with a colorful blooming flower box, separating entrance and exit, looked sedate and simple. But when she opened the door to the most sparkling, modern, opulent waiting room she'd ever seen, she blinked. Gray-and-black marble floors, white leather chairs, a crystal pedestal beneath a glass table in the center with a fuchsia-colored chandelier above it, nearly took her breath away.

A young and attractive blonde woman sat in one of the seats, quietly thumbing through a fashion magazine. Next to her, a middle-aged redhead, showing the results of some recent facial surgery, watched Grace's every move.

She walked to the front desk, where another middle-aged, beautifully coiffed woman, with a name badge that said Helen, Senior Receptionist waited with a smile. Grace gave her name and her reason for being there, then turned to take a seat. She barely had time to sit in one of those amazing chairs or read the long list of surgeons' names on the wall when the dashing Leo Hunter himself opened a door and invited her inside. Where had he been last night?

Tall, with longish black hair that flipped out a little under his ear lobes, sparkling, ocean-blue eyes, and a totally fit-looking frame, he was a man who obviously turned a lot of heads when he walked down the street. At least, he'd already turned hers, plus those of the two other ladies sharing the waiting room, though she hoped her obvious appreciation of his great looks wasn't as obvious as theirs.

The dashing surgeon offered a welcoming smile. Great teeth, too! "Grace, it's a pleasure to meet you."

"Thank you. Nice to meet you, too. Sorry I missed you last night. I had a good time, though."

He took a beat to think before those gorgeous eyes lit up. "Oh, the fund-raiser. Glad you enjoyed it. Yes, well, I had a great excuse—making honeymoon plans with the busiest travel agent in London."

"How wonderful. Congratulations."

They shook hands and he showed her into his office, gesturing for her to sit as he rounded his huge walnut desk and took his seat. "You're going to love it here, and I've been eagerly awaiting your arrival." He shuffled papers around while she sat.

"Thank you. I'm very excited about getting started myself."

Leo settled down and rested one hand on top of the other at his desk. "You've come highly recommended, you know. And what you did for those childhood cancer survivors in Arizona—reconstructing their faces, noses and jaws—well, I was blown away by your talent. That's when I knew I wanted, no, needed someone of your caliber here at our clinic."

Overcome with his compliments, she felt a blush coming on. She'd worn a thin white turtleneck under her spring-blue blazer. Maybe she'd have a fighting chance to cover up the warmth as it started on her chest and worked its way up her neck and cheeks before blossoming into pink. "You're too kind, Mr. Hunter."

"Call me Leo, please."

"Leo," she practiced, knowing that out of respect for him and his world-renowned clinic, it would probably never come easily to her.

"We have weekly staff meetings to discuss our various cases, and we share notes from both our successes and challenges. The point is to keep growing and learning. Don't you agree?"

"Wholeheartedly. That's why I accepted your generous offer to work here." She wouldn't go into the fact about needing to get away from her stuck-in-first-gear life.

He flashed that charming smile again and stood. "What do you say I give you a tour of our clinic? You'll have an office here as well, of course, plus scheduled procedures, but you'll be doing your more complicated surgeries at Princess Catherine's or the Lighthouse Children's hospitals, like everyone else."

She nodded as he came round the desk again and directed her out of his office door.

"I'll introduce you to some of the staff. Unfortunately, a lot of them are in Theater this morning."

He walked her further down the long, pristine hall, with original artwork hanging on the walls, stunning her with color and beauty. Not a single comfort had been spared in this clinic.

He popped his head inside an office. It was empty. He respected the privacy of all occupied procedure rooms, but announced himself then tugged her inside the staff lounge. A half dozen nurses greeted her with genuine smiles, and she felt warmly welcomed and thought maybe she'd finally found a place where she could belong.

Though most of the office doors were closed, she saw the nameplates on them: Iain McKenzie, Rafael de Luca, Edward North, Abbie de Luca, Declan Underwood, Kara Stephens. The hallway forked in another direction, with more names on the office doors. All closed. Then around the corner, at the far end, was another closed door. The plaque read Ethan Hunter, his office as far away from his brother's office as possible in this building.

"Sorry things look a bit like a ghost town today, but we keep a heavy schedule. Mondays are always busy and everyone is either in Theater or preparing to do surgery."

"I understand."

A chirpy female voice came from another office as they doubled back.

"Oh, at least I can introduce you to Alexia Robbins. Lexi, as we call her. She's our head of public relations." He tapped on the partially open door. "Lexi?"

She was on the phone, but immediately waved them in while she quickly finished up her conversation. "Great, I'll have all the information to you by this afternoon. Thanks!"

She hung up and looked excitedly at Leo. "Just scored a two-minute promo on the local news station about yesterday's charity event at the Eye." She stopped talking when she realized Leo wasn't alone.

"Fantastic," he said. "Tell me all about it later."

"Will do."

"Lexi, this is Grace Turner, our newest reconstructive surgeon."

"Oh, lovely to meet you." Lexi jumped to her feet and offered her hand. They shook lightly. Grace immediately liked the tall, bubbly lady with blonde hair and an hourglass figure, wearing a bright pink dress. Her flashing blue eyes gave off a mischievous glint. "If there's anything I can do to help in any way..."

"As a matter of fact," Leo said, "I was hoping you'd give her a tour of the hospitals this afternoon."

"Love to."

"Grand. Talk later." Leo moved toward the door.

"Hold on, mister," Lexi said playfully. "How is the honeymoon planning going?"

Leo gave her a look. She wouldn't back down. "Well?"

"What do you think, Lexi? I've married the most wonderful girl in the world. Paris in June will be perfect."

Lexi's cheeks pinkened with pleasure. She nearly sighed, like a woman in love. Leo glanced at Grace, who was feeling very out of the loop.

"Lexi recently got engaged herself, so she's being a busybody."

"It's my job, being in PR and all," she teased back, playing with the ring band...which held a huge rock. Wow.

Grace had never seen anything like it. Whatever the stone, it was humongous and pink, and all the little surrounding diamonds sparkled around it.

"So what do you say, Grace, is noon good for you?" Lexi tore Grace away from her thoughts. "We can grab lunch at the clinic buffet before we head over to the hospitals."

"Sounds good. Thank you."

Off Leo and Grace went, retracing their steps along the row of closed doors. "We do a lot of our plastics on-site. Down there is the recovery room. Plus we make arrangements for many of our patients to spend the night in nearby luxury recovery apartments," he said.

She'd gotten the impression many of the first-floor apartments in her building were there for that very reason.

"I've put you next to another American. Wanted to make you feel at home."

He opened the door and showed her the beautifully decorated office that would be hers. It was small but comfortable with a lovely window that let in daylight. She turned in a circle looking at everything, thinking how she'd utilize the space, cabinets and amazing medical library. She went behind her chrome-and-glass desk and tested out the white leather chair. "I love it."

"Wonderful." Leo leaned against the doorframe. "Cooper! Come out and meet your new neighbor," Leo called into the hallway, then looked back at her. "I'm glad you like it. You'll get along swimmingly with Mitchell Cooper. He's one of our top plastic surgeons. Been with us four years now." Leo smiled at someone outside in the hallway. "Come and meet Grace Turner. She's American, too."

Popping into the doorway, sporting a wide grin, adventurous pod man appeared. And Grace nearly fell out of her custom comfort chair.

She looked at him. He stared back. Both of them were wide-eyed and unbelieving. A silent message jumped between them, followed by a quick bargain. Leo wouldn't find out that they'd already met. Agreed.

"Grace, meet Mitchell Cooper."

Mustering every ounce of poise she owned, Grace stood and stretched out her hand. "It's a pleasure to meet you, Mitchell."

He accepted her proffered hand and shook it. "The pleasure's all mine. Welcome to Harley Street." Quick memories of how she'd squeezed his hand in the cab, just before he'd bussed her cheek, caught her off guard.

A large cat must have hovered over the office, taking their tongues as heavy silence overtook the room. Leo glanced between the two of them, as if trying to figure out what had just happened. "Do you two already know each other?"

"No!" they said in unison, exchanging surreptitious glances.

Leo didn't look convinced, but didn't press it. "Well, I'll leave you alone to get acquainted, then. You can talk Dodger dogs and touchdowns, or whatever it is Americans…" His voice trailed off as he headed for the door then turned on his heel. "We've got some major cases coming in and we'll be utilizing your skills and talents right off, Grace. I've left the first one on your desk." He glanced at Mitchell. "And I think you'll make a great team on the Cumberbatch case, too." Then he was off.

The silence grew nearly deafening as Grace stared at Mitch in disbelief, not knowing whether to be happy or regretful that she'd seen him again. What if he was in a serious relationship with someone, and he'd strayed a little last night? How awkward. From the caution in his eyes, Grace settled on the regretful side of the scale.

"Look," he said, "I had no idea you were our new surgeon." He grabbed his head. "Stupid, stupid, stupid. I should have put things together."

"I didn't offer any information either."

"I should have asked, but I got this crazy idea about having a minivacation with Madam X." He made air quotes with his fingers around the name. "For crying out loud, I apologize." He looked seriously sorry, too.

"There's nothing to apologize for. I had fun. I

don't know about you, but I did, anyway." She leaned against the edge of her desk.

"Yes. Of course it was fun. But the thing is, I never would have treated you that way if I'd known you were the new team member."

"Then I'm glad you didn't know."

"It's just bad business on my part. Bad form." His hands rested on his trim hips. She couldn't help but notice.

He wore a starched white shirt and blue Paisley-patterned tie to complement his navy slacks. His knee-length doctor's coat covered all of his best parts, as she recalled—the wide shoulders and strong arms—arms that had lifted her nearly over the fence without effort.

"Stop it," she said. "We did what we did. Now we forget about it and get professional. That's all. It's not like we had sex or anything."

An impish gleam entered his wonderfully green eyes. Thank goodness he remembered the fun they'd had. "But we're pod people. Young adventurers. How do we forget that?"

She couldn't help it. He'd tried to lighten the

mood and successfully made her laugh. Were all women like putty in his hands? "Stop it."

She searched for something and ineptly threw a piece of paper from her desk at him. A sorry weapon, it floated nowhere near where he stood. He pretended to dodge it anyway. "But I suppose we'll always have that." She fought back the urge to laugh more, liking him for bringing it up.

He raised and dropped his brows. "Just two peas in a pod."

That did it. She sputtered a laugh, and he joined her. "Stop it, I said."

He shook his head, looking chagrined. "I broke up with you." He pinched the bridge of his nose and grimaced. "Do you realize I had the audacity to pick you up in a pod, nearly get you arrested in a public playground, buy you dinner on a barstool, then send you home in a cab, hardly explaining why I could never see you again? I'm an idiot. What in the hell must you think of me?"

She wanted to say she'd thought about him the rest of the night. She'd thought about him as she'd showered and dressed for work today, too, and the word *idiot* had never come into the mix. But she knew better.

They needed to forget their extraordinary night out and move on to reality. They were colleagues now. They'd have to see each other every day, and it was never a good idea to get involved with a coworker, especially in such a small clinic like this. They needed to keep their distance from each other, leave well enough alone. It was so obvious.

Just because he'd said he was divorced last night, it didn't mean he was a free man. He probably had half a dozen kids he needed to divide all of his spare time among. But look at that, he was staring at her legs, and since she'd worn a high-waisted pencil skirt, there was plenty of leg to stare at. She crossed her ankles and pretended not to notice.

He'd sent her home in that cab for a good reason, and there was no point in dredging it up now. "What I think of you doesn't matter any more because we're colleagues and I've already had my first case assigned to me. From now on we're strictly business. Okay?"

It was safe, too, since she'd never shown her

scars to a man who wasn't one of her doctors. Except for her ex-fiancé, and what a disaster that had turned out to be. How could she possibly venture into a relationship with anyone, no matter how well and easily they got along, when no man would ever want her. Boy, she'd certainly jumped ahead…. What was it about Mitchell Cooper that made her want to?

His tentative expression turned thoughtful. He was obviously working through the steps on how to undo a perfectly wonderful evening with a woman he'd never expected to see again but who was now his office mate, too. "Okay. Makes sense. Strictly business partners. Got it. Probably for the best anyway."

She spotted that same look he'd left her with last night, and she'd interpreted it—projected her own feelings into it—as regret. That truly was how she felt, and that's how life was sometimes—loaded with regret. And secrets best not shared.

He took her hand and shook again. "Nice to meet you, Grace Turner. If you need any 'strictly professional' help, I'll be right next door." With that, he turned and left.

* * *

Mitch wanted to kick the hallway wall. He'd botched up a perfectly good partnership, making his new colleague feel uncomfortable and regretting ever having laid eyes on him. The thing was, he'd really, really liked her, and it had taken every last kernel of restraint not to ask for her phone number last night, even though on the surface she wasn't the kind of mommy material he had in mind.

But as always, before he'd been able to get the words out, the pain he'd endured from his wife choosing his best friend over him had strangled the thought out of him. He needed to forget about women for a while, especially beautiful women, and focus on what mattered most in his life—his daughter, Mia, and his job.

Some flaw in his ex's self-esteem had turned her into a plastic-surgery addict, even though she'd been beautiful to begin with. Now he hardly recognized her doll-like appearance. And he was damned if he'd let that weakness be a constant example for his Mia. He'd moved as far away as possible four years ago, once they'd divorced and Christie had given him full custody of their daughter.

Those were the things he needed to focus on—his reason for being at this clinic, and for moving to London. A better life for Mia. Not the beautiful and fun-loving Grace Turner next door. A man was an idiot if he didn't learn from his mistakes.

He plopped into his desk chair and tried desperately to get her crystal-blue eyes and especially her gorgeous mouth out of his mind. Damn. And after several moments of wrestling with his thoughts, he resolved to keep Grace at arm's length. For his own good.

He'd given up beautiful women, had only dated stable potential-mother material after his first failed relationship on moving to London four years ago. He'd gotten himself involved too soon with one of the Hunter Clinic nurses right off. That had turned into a disaster with the nurse leaving the clinic rather than work with him once they'd broken up. So far the process of sticking with mommy material had been a huge failure, but he'd keep on. It was the only way. Nothing would stop him from finding a proper mother for Mia.

But knowing Grace was on the other side of their adjoining office wall would make deleting her from his personal life as difficult as—he fished around on his desk for the surgical referral of his next patient—making Mrs. Evermore look twenty years younger, which was her surgical goal on the application for a face-lift.

Grace spent the afternoon with Lexi on a tour of the two state-of-the-art hospitals where she'd be authorized to perform surgery. The Lighthouse Children's Hospital was merely ten minutes away, and Princess Catherine's was beautifully placed alongside the Thames with magnificent views from most patients' rooms.

Lexi was a natural conversationalist so Grace didn't feel pressured to talk much.

"If you'd like, we're meeting for drinks at Drake's wine bar after work tonight," she said. "I'm bringing pictures of my dream dress for my wedding day. Now all I have to do is find a way to pay for it!" She laughed.

"Well, I can't miss that, now, can I?" Thinking about the pristine and lonely apartment, Grace agreed to meet at the wine bar, as Lexi had described it.

"Great. We'll go together." They got into an elevator with a glass wall to allow the full view of the river Thames all the way down. "Oh, and the shoes I've got in mind are to die for. Of course, I might have to pawn the ring to buy both." She beamed and poofed her hair.

Grace smiled, adoring the lady's spirit.

Before she left the hospital, Grace met the man who'd be the lead surgical nurse on her team, Ron Whidbey, a middle-aged man of African descent who'd been born and raised in England.

Her first case—reconstructing a face, status postcancer resection—was one that Mitchell would be involved in as well, as the twenty-five-year-old woman would need new lips. Apparently, that was his specialty. As for herself, she'd concentrate on reconstructing the nose and cheeks and recreating a philtrum in preparation for Mitchell's side of the operation.

Tomorrow, during surgery, she'd be so focused

on her patient she'd probably not even notice Mitchell was there. A girl could hope anyway.

After a long discussion with Ron about what instruments and setup she preferred and how she liked to approach reconstructive surgery, she felt they were both on the same page and had a firm understanding of how it would be working together. He promised to meet her in O.R. Six at Kate's, as the locals liked to call Princess Catherine's, at 6:00 a.m. sharp with the room set up and ready to go per her orders. Then off he went to have a meeting with his nursing team.

At 6:00 p.m., having not seen hide nor hair of Mitchell for the rest of the day, Grace heard a tap at her door. It was Lexi, keeping her promise to take her to Drake's wine bar, at the Regent's Park end of Harley Street. Within fifteen minutes she was sitting in what resembled a classic Victorian chamber with crystal chandeliers and overstuffed benches and booths, amidst dark colors and dim lights.

Surrounded by several of her new colleagues, she'd been served a glass of crisp, unoaked Chardonnay, and as happy as a lark she munched on crackers, cheese puffs, veggies with hummus dip and mixed nuts.

Across from her, Lexi's fiancé, Iain, a fellow reconstructive surgeon who'd been working at the Hunter Clinic for the last few years, draped his long, muscular arm about Lexi's hip and the woman seemed to no longer need a drink. Several of the nursing staff were also there. A chestnut-haired woman sidled her way between Edward North, the stiff but gifted microsurgeon, and another nursing colleague, then introduced herself to Grace as Charlotte. They chatted about the weather and the surgeries the clinic undertook. Since Grace had been watching and waiting for Mitchell to show up, she said a little prayer of thanks for the welcome distraction with Charlotte.

Next, Lexi gathered all the ladies at one end of the bar. Grace joined them.

"Look what I've got." Lexi whipped out a picture of a divine designer dress torn from a fashion magazine. "Isn't it gorgeous? This is what I intend to wear the day I get married."

A couple of nurses squealed over the dress.

Charlotte was one of them. Grace had to admit the pink chiffon with ribbon waistband and decorative sequins was a sight to behold. She glanced at Lexi, who was transfixed, along with the nurses. She obviously liked pink, judging by the dress she'd worn today, and pink was certainly her color.

"Now the only problem is hunting down a good knockoff because there's no way on earth I can afford this one."

"If anyone can do it, you can, Lexi," Charlotte said.

Grace smiled. "Good luck. Something tells me you'll find your dream dress at the right price."

"From your lips to the shopping goddess's ears," Lexi said. Once she'd put the picture away, the nurses went off to the ladies room, and Grace followed Lexi back to the Hunter Clinic corner of the bar.

Glancing around the extremely attractive group of people, Grace thought good looks might be part of the job requirement to be employed at Hunter Clinic, but then wondered why she'd been hired.

Though the clinic group seemed tight knit, they went out of their way to make her feel a part of things. She'd just about finished her drink and was feeling relaxed, and as she was performing surgery in the morning decided she wouldn't have another. She asked the server to bring her a glass of water and just as she looked up, in walked Mitchell. Their eyes locked briefly, long enough to set off flutters in her chest, and he went straightaway to the bar to order a drink.

Every time she saw him her heart stumbled over beats. How could a guy like that not be involved with anyone? She watched the door for a lady to follow him inside, but no one came. Just about the time her water arrived, and another Hunter Clinic surgeon named Declan Underwood was deep into explaining rugby to her, Mitch swaggered up with a beer in hand.

"Evening, all," he said.

Everyone called out some greeting or other.

"Lips!" Iain said, and Grace wondered if it bothered Mitch to have such a nickname, though she did understand men loved to gibe each other like that. In fact, in her psychology classes in med school she'd learned that kind of behavior was a sign of affection—something most men would never be caught dead admitting.

She found it hard to concentrate and simply nodded hello when Mitch approached.

"May I sit here?" he asked, pointing to the barely six inches of padded bench next to her.

"Of course," she said, scooting closer to Lexi. Avoiding Mitchell Cooper was out of the question now, so she decided to get used to it right off. Crammed in next to her, she felt the warmth radiate from his body, and caught the scent of the same tangy, expensive aftershave that had lingered in the cab the other night. What should she do now?

"How was your first day?" he said.

"Fine. After the shock wore off."

He caught his lower lip with his teeth and nodded. "There's a lot of names and faces to put together," he said, not letting on he'd understood her true meaning of "shock," which had nothing to do with meeting the staff.

"Yes. That's for sure." How inane could their conversation get? It had flowed so easily last night, when they'd been strangers. She longed for the clock to turn back twenty-four hours.

He reached for a handful of nuts and crammed them in his mouth. So much for continuing the conversation.

Lexi appeared in front of them. "Iain and I are leaving early," she said to Grace.

From the way the couple had had their hands all over each other, Grace didn't need to be told the reason why they wanted to leave early. She smiled.

"Can we drop you off?" Iain asked.

Grace waited for Mitchell to offer to take her home, but after half a beat, when he hadn't volunteered, she stood.

"Thanks, I'd love that," she said. "Good night, everybody. It was great to meet all of you."

"You'll see everyone else at Friday's staff meeting," someone called out, but she was so distracted by Mitch and now her leaving that she wasn't even sure who'd said it.

"See you in surgery tomorrow, Mitchell."

He nodded.

Everyone else smiled and cheered her off,

while Mitchell still chomped on his mouthful of mixed nuts, watching, looking clueless and disinterested, and nothing like the adventurous pod person she'd met last night. At least he'd kept his word—from now on theirs would be a strictly business relationship.

The next morning, at a quarter to six, Grace scrubbed in. It was a process she preferred to do by herself, since the short-sleeved scrub top revealed a large portion of her scars. But gowning was different. She needed help to do it properly. Grace caught the quick, surprised glimpse in the scrub nurse's eyes as she helped her don the sterile gown and gloves, and tried to act as if nothing was unusual.

Once her mask was in place, she used her shoulder to push the plate for the automatic door opener to the surgical suite. Happy to make eye contact with Ron right off, she saw him nod, and from the squint of his dark eyes above the mask, she knew he smiled beneath.

She assessed her O.R. A quick check of the instruments satisfied her strict stipulations. The anesthesiologist began to put the mildly sedated patient completely under right after Grace had introduced herself. Two nurses were on hand to assist with the operation, and once she'd done the lion's share of the surgery, Mitchell would step in to create the actual lips for the young woman. She hadn't seen him this morning, but had been told he was on the premises and would wait to enter the O.R. until needed. It relieved Grace, knowing he wouldn't be looking over her shoulder. She couldn't allow a single distraction in her O.R.

Cancer had claimed most of the patient's face, and after the dermatologist had made wide resections of the mass, very little was left of her nose or upper lip. It broke Grace's heart, suspecting the twenty-five-year-old patient felt more like a monster than human with a hole for her nose, and gums showing where her upper lip should have been. When Grace had first been burned, before the multiple skin grafts, she'd felt like a monster, too. Her job today was to put the woman back together again. The young woman's face would never look as it once had, but at least she'd have a face she wouldn't be ashamed to show in public.

Grace would have to borrow cartilage from her ears to rebuild portions of the bridge and nose tip, and take bilateral transpositional flaps from her cheeks to cover the nose, reconstruct the natural curvature of the nasal rim, and create the missing upper lip. After she'd finished the general rebuilding, Mitchell would make a more natural-looking mouth by using treated fat transfer from the patient's abdomen.

"Let's give Julie Treadwell a beautiful new face, shall we?" she said. Everyone present nodded. "Scalpel," she said, then made her first incision.

An hour and a half later, up to her elbows in blood, cartilage and skin flaps, one lone straggler entered the O.R. She knew it wasn't the circulating nurse, because she hadn't requested anything. She'd just made two small labial folds on either side of the nose flap, and had asked for the small curved needle and sutures to stitch everything in place.

She glanced up. It was him.

Knowing Mitch Cooper was there made her

hand tense slightly, but only for a brief second. The patient deserved one hundred percent of her attention. She waited until she'd recovered her concentration to put the finishing touches on her portion of this two-stage surgery.

When she'd finished, she handed the patient over to Mitch then prepared to step outside to watch him work his wonders.

"Stick around," he said. "You might learn something."

She smiled at his teasing—now, that was more like the guy she remembered. "Wouldn't want to get in the way."

"You won't. Besides, I might need to pick your brain on some of the trickier parts. From the looks of Ms. Treadwell, you've done a fantastic job, Miss Turner."

Why his compliment meant so much, she couldn't fathom, but it did. Going against her instinct to leave the good surgeon to his work, she accepted his invitation and stuck around.

Mitch took his time making sure everything was exactly as he needed it to be. Grace had already laid down the framework preserving the intraoral mucosal lining. Now he worked to maintain the oral aperture. The entire procedure would require a three-layer closure of mucosa, muscle and skin with tiny drains inserted. It couldn't be rushed.

He'd originally planned on making a traditional mouth—a serviceable mouth. Anything would be better than the completely missing lips that the patient currently had. But since Grace had blown into town, he couldn't get a certain styled mouth out of his mind, and he thought he'd give that style a go. The classic and beautiful Grace Turner mouth. If all went well, he'd duplicate it on Julie Treadwell.

Mitch worked his wonders, creating a cupid's bow for the upper lip, then using the autograft flap from the donor site—the delicate radial forearm epidermis—for best match to the facial skin. If the patient desired more color to her lips, he'd suggest she have them tinted once everything was healed. But that was down the line. His job today was to create the size and shape of the lips.

He glanced up over his surgical magnifying

glasses at Grace, but realized he'd have to work completely from memory as she wore her O.R. mask.

"Pass the syringe," he said, once everything had been accomplished as planned. His surgical nurse knew exactly what he wanted and handed him the syringe with the treated fat from Julie's abdomen. Meticulously, he injected the material along the path he'd just created with the tender fasciocutaneous flap, and carefully manipulated it into place. Everything had to be just so to form the perfect amount of plumpness, and he couldn't waste any of the prepared fat. He would continue until every last bit of it had been used.

If all went well, tomorrow morning Julie Treadwell would be the proud owner of a replica of Grace Turner's luscious lips.

Over the last hour, Grace had developed new respect for, and maybe a tiny crush on, Mitch Cooper and his skills as a cosmetic plastic surgeon.

When the surgery was complete, she complimented him then rushed off to dispose of her surgical gown and headed for the women doctors' lounge. Pride made her do it before Mitch had a chance to see the angry scars on her arms, chest and neck.

They met up later at the patient's bedside, after she'd left Recovery and was back in her room. Grace was dressed in a pale blue long-sleeved turtleneck underneath a gray pinstriped vest and matching slacks—scars safely covered, so no one would know. "How's our patient doing?" she asked Mitch, who'd beat her there.

"Really well." He finished rebandaging Julie's face. "No excess bleeding. No early signs of infection. Minimal edema. All drains intact." He glanced up at her. "The reconstruction is really superb."

There was admiration in those intense green eyes, and Grace fought off the urge to puff up her feathers. "That's great. I'd hate to make you unwrap her again, so I'll take your word for it. But tomorrow I get first dibs at the bandages."

"Roger that." He casually saluted above the sleeping patient. "Now, if you'd like, follow me, and I'll show you the staff cafeteria."

Did she want to spend time alone with him

again? Her first reaction was no, it would just make her wish things were different. But Mitch was already heading toward the door, and truth was her stomach had grumbled just before she'd entered the patient's room. She was hungry. He knew where the food was. She'd be stupid not to follow him.

Before she left Julie's bedside, she took the young woman's hand in hers and squeezed it. "You were a great patient today, Julie. I'm so happy how things turned out." She spoke knowing that, even though the patient looked asleep, hearing was the last of the senses to go under and the first to wake up. Julie lightly squeezed Grace's hand back and it made Grace smile. Julie had heard every word she'd just said.

Grace gently brushed a few errant tendrils of hair away from the bandages and looked hard into her covered face. She imagined how much better Julie would look when next she gazed into the mirror, and smiled. "Get some rest, Julie. It's been a long day and the worst is over."

Julie mumbled something but was already pushing through to the other side of consciousness.

Grace glanced up and noticed an odd expression on Mitchell's face. She smiled, and he gave a reverent nod.

The ride down in the elevator was awkward. After running out of compliments to give each other for the successful surgery, there wasn't much else to talk about as she chose to keep things strictly professional with Mitchell. As had he, which was obvious from his actions last night.

She saw him start to say something, or at least she thought that was what he'd meant by taking a quick breath and opening his mouth. But he bit his lips closed, as if thinking better of starting any kind of casual conversation. Again, they were on the same page. Two adventurous pod people long forgotten. Finally, they arrived in the basement and as soon as the doors opened the aroma from several different dishes had her stomach growling happily in response.

Fortunately, several other doctors were in the cafeteria, and after she and Mitch got their food, they sat in two completely different spots at the large table. When Mitch had introduced Grace, a handful of the other doctors greeted her and engaged her in conversation. Only occasionally did her eyes drift Mitch's way, and from time to time their gazes connected. Each time they both quickly glanced away, but not before a small burst of something happened in her chest.

She took the last bite of her Cobb salad while wishing he didn't affect her like that, but her mental desires and those of her body currently seemed to be on two completely different tracks.

The next morning, before Grace began her appointments at the Hunter Clinic, she took a cab to Kate's to visit Julie Treadwell. She'd thought about her most of the night, hoping and praying the surgery had put her back together well enough that she could deal with her new identity, hold her head high, and move on with her life.

One of the nurses smiled at her just before she entered Julie's room, and Grace returned the gesture, immediately recognizing her. The ward nurse was Charlotte, the attractive woman Grace had met at Drake's last night.

Julie sat up in bed, her facial bandages intact.

The TV was on a fun, chatty morning show. She sucked a protein shake with added vitamins and minerals through a straw. Grace knew exactly what it was because she'd requested it in her post-op orders.

"Hi, Julie, how are you feeling today?"

"Not too bad. A bit like a mummy, but I know it's part of the package."

Grace smiled. "I don't want to disturb you, but I'd like to change your bandages."

Julie put down the drink immediately. "Sure." Her hands fisted in her lap. Grace could only imagine how nerve-racking waiting to see your new face would be.

"I'll let the nurse know what I need, then we'll get started, okay?"

Julie nodded bravely.

When Grace returned after asking Charlotte for the items she'd need, she had a hard bargain of which to convince Julie, "I'd like to suggest that you don't look at your face until most of the swelling and bruising has gone down. Maybe in a few days. Are you okay with that?"

"I'm not ready to look just yet anyway."

Grace took one of Julie's hands, the fist loosening as she reached for it, and squeezed. "You've been through a lot with the cancer. We'll take this one step at a time." Julie's eyes filled and brimmed with tears.

Charlotte brought in the new dressing materials, and Grace pulled the bedside curtains closed and got started cutting the gauze with her bandage scissors. She'd decided to keep this dressing change between her and the patient. She started at the forehead and carefully worked her way down from there.

Once some of the dressings came loose, she made a point of schooling her expression, of not showing any reaction to what she saw. Yes, Julie looked stitched up like a quilt, and the post-op edema distorted her features, but overall Grace was very happy with her appearance. As things settled down, the swelling would lessen and the stitches would dissolve or come out, and Julie would look human again. Her nose looked great. Grace continued snipping away at the bandages while thinking and planning. After Julie was completely healed, Grace would discuss erasing some of the remaining scars through laser treatments.

In fact, she'd already talked to Leo Hunter about having a few treatments on a particularly troublesome scar near her neck herself. Laser treatments had worked wonders for many of her patients; why shouldn't she try them?

She came to the upper-lip portion of the surgery and was very pleased with her work and almost smiled, then finished removing the remaining gauze. Mitchell's lip job looked superb...and strangely familiar. He'd gone beyond the call of duty and augmented Julie's lower lip as well, to make them match up in the best way possible.

The upper lip picked up where her philtrum groove left off in what she'd describe as a classic cupid's bow. He'd plumped up the lower lip, but hadn't overdone it. These lips looked as natural as hers.

The oddest feeling came over Grace while looking at the au fait mouth. Where had she seen that style of mouth before? She smiled. Coming from Hollywood, the talented Mitchell Cooper had probably duplicated some famous starlet's lips just for Julie.

CHAPTER THREE

FRIDAY MORNING THE entire staff of Hunter Clinic gathered at eight a.m. for the weekly staff meeting in the large and luxurious employee lounge. Grace took a seat beside Ron Whidbey and pediatric surgeon Abbie de Luca.

"We've had a very busy week," Leo said, taking charge, glancing at a printout, "with another full schedule for next week." He looked up and scanned the entire group. "I've heard some concerns about being overbooked, yet no one has come to me to complain. Though there has been evidence of people still crashing on the couch in my office."

He cleared his throat. That got a laugh that rippled around the room, and Ethan looked especially guilty, scratching the back of his neck and looking at the ceiling. "So if you're feeling you need some time off, make an appointment and we'll talk about it." He looked specifically at the nursing staff. "I don't want to overextend any of you."

Grace glanced around the room, but didn't see Mitch. An odd mix of relief and disappointment confused her. *Make up your mind, you're either interested or not. Sheesh.*

Leo then picked up a notepad and read from his planned notes.

"There have been some reports of staph infections in another London clinic. I've hired an infectious-diseases specialist to tour and assess our procedure rooms, even though we haven't had any such outbreak. I just want to be careful. So if you see a man with glasses and white hair wandering about, that will be Dr. Richard Thornswood. As always, we expect everyone to practice meticulous sterile technique, and Lizzie will have a separate meeting with our environmental-services staff to make sure they are also following all safeguards to the T with cleaning, disinfecting, and disposal."

Next, Leo invited Rafael de Luca to bring everyone up to date with a short talk on the latest developments in identifying and treating cleft palate in vitro.

Grace was transfixed by the level of knowledge of everyone on staff. Her concentration was soon interrupted, though, when Mitchell made a late entry and took a nearby seat.

No longer able to concentrate on what Rafael was talking about, she became totally aware of Mitch sitting to her right, one row forward. The vantage point gave her the chance to study his rich dark hair, how it waved ever so gently along his neck and kissed the collar of his forest-green shirt. She could only imagine how green his eyes would look with that shirt—

"Grace, would you like to stand up?" Leo said, jolting her out of her pleasant dream state.

"Oh, yes, certainly." She stood and waited expectantly.

Leo gazed at her as if it was her turn to talk, but as she hadn't been paying attention for a few seconds, admiring Cooper and his glorious hair instead, she didn't have a clue what he wanted.

Feeling a blush on her cheeks, she decided to

come clean. "I'm sorry, what did you want me to do?"

A few people chuckled, and that made her feel embarrassed and nervous. She cast a lightning glance at Mitch and found his sweet, sympathetic smile, and calmed the slightest bit.

"I just wanted to introduce you to those who haven't had a chance to meet you yet. Why don't you tell us a little about your background?"

With that, she composed herself and told her history in as short and concise a way as possible. Hating to be put in the spotlight, she forced a benign smile and pretended she enjoyed this exercise in awkwardness.

She'd worn a red mandarin-collared silk top with black slacks today, and her doctor's coat covered her arms. She didn't need to worry about her scars showing. Leo Hunter was the only person at Hunter Clinic who knew about her condition, and had even promised to take a look at the problematic scar above her clavicle after the staff meeting.

"We heard your first surgery went splendidly," Leo said, prodding her along.

"Oh, yes, thanks in no small part to Mr. Cooper." She smiled at him.

"Lips, lips, lips," Iain chanted, making everyone titter.

Evidently Mitch had quite a reputation.

Her gaze landed on Mitchell, who looked nonplussed by the teasing. He sat straight, ignoring Iain, instead smiling at her, as if silently cheering her on. She couldn't help but think about Julie Treadwell's surgery. She'd racked her brain on where she'd seen that mouth before, how similar it looked to her own when she'd studied herself in the mirror. Was he really that talented, or was it a wild coincidence that she was making far, far too much of? Of course it was.

When she'd finished her introduction, she nodded gratefully to Mitch. Shortly, after a few more announcements, Leo dismissed the meeting. Mitch stood and turned, looking right at her. In her gut she wanted him to come over and talk to her, but she felt a tap on her shoulder.

It was Leo. "I've got time to fix that issue we spoke about. Shall we go to a procedure room?"

"Oh, that would be great. Thanks," she said, seizing the moment.

She followed Leo out of the room, but before leaving she glanced back and couldn't help noticing a disturbed expression on Mitchell's face. Surely he wasn't jealous of a man who'd just gotten married?

Mitch overheard Leo invite Grace to a procedure room, and he watched them leave together. His heart sank. Was she having a little nip, tuck or Botox? Perhaps all three? Damn, he'd been so sure she'd never had anything done. His stomach went a little queasy over the thought of Grace having treatments done at such a young age. Little things led to bigger treatments, then more nips and tucks and more often. Bile soured his throat.

Her beauty was natural, and should stay that way. He knew too well the sad story of women chasing their youth, one procedure at a time, until they wound up looking nothing like their former selves. Hell, he had a thirty-five-year-old patient with cat eyes and a tympanic-drum-stretched face scheduled for a knee lift this very afternoon to prove his point.

"Hey, Lips." Declan Underwood slapped Mitch on the back. The rugby-playing plastic surgeon nearly knocked him off balance.

He clicked into his office persona. "Hey, man, how's your weekend shaping up?"

"Great. Got a couple of games lined up tomorrow. You should bring Mia out to watch."

"Only if you can promise no blood or gore."

"Can't do that. Besides, my rugby team brings the clinic a lot of business."

"True. So true." He'd fixed a broken nose on more than a few of Declan's teammates over the last year. One guy with a caved-in forehead had been sent to the emergency room for more extensive exams. The last he heard, they'd had to drain a hematoma between his skull and brain.

Declan tipped his head toward the door through which Leo and Grace had just exited. "She's hot, don't you think?"

A new feeling displaced the caution and concern about her having a procedure done with Leo.

Jealousy. Wow, just like that, red flames of anger shot up his spine.

He stiffened. "She's definitely a knockout," he said between clenched teeth. He was at work, talking to a colleague, he had to play along and not let on how he really felt.

The men smiled at each other in appreciation for the opposite sex in general. But, damn, Mitch couldn't let it go.

"Just one more thing, Declan."

Declan raised his dark brows in anticipation.

"I saw her first."

Now added to the wild stew of emotions simmering through him, Mitch had thrown total confusion into the pot. Hadn't his last office relationship ended in disaster? If he was looking for mommy material, he needed to stick with his plan, no matter how bored he was with the process.

Did he want Grace? Or did he want to run as far and as fast as he could away from her? At some point he'd have to make up his mind.

"Message received, Lips," Declan said, wandering off, giving the appearance of not being the least bit offended.

* * *

Six days later, having done a fantastic job of not seeing Mitch since last Friday's staff meeting—thanks to conflicting O.R. and clinic schedules and well-planned avoidance techniques—Grace stayed late at work to catch up on some paperwork.

The laser procedure Leo had performed on the buckling scar on her chest was smoothing out and healing beautifully, and she thought about asking him to touch up a few other spots in the near future.

Her phone rang.

She answered, and the person introduced herself.

The Cumberbatch case she'd been assigned on her very first day at the Hunter Clinic was proving to be high profile.

She was surprised that the call was from a tabloid journalist with a long list of questions about Britain's favorite bad-boy punk rocker. She refused to disclose anything and soon as she hung up needed someone to bounce her concerns off.

Sitting in her office that late Thursday afternoon, knowing Mitch was just around the corner—because she'd heard his door open not less than a half hour ago—she decided to finally pay him a visit. After all, she'd been at the Hunter Clinic going on two weeks and he was her next-door neighbor. Yes, they'd seen each other at the staff meeting last Friday but hadn't spoken to each other, just passed a meaningful glance or two each other's way. It was high time she popped in…for a strictly business matter.

She took an extra few moments to smooth her hair, which she'd worn down today. She checked her make-up, or what was left of it, and applied a new layer of lipstick. Then she retied the colorful scarf she wore with a double-loop wrap around her neck, loose yet high enough to cover her scars. She'd skipped her usual turtleneck today and wore a long-sleeved, boat-necked, white silk top over her black straight-legged slacks, so she needed that scarf. Besides brightening up the outfit, the scarf also picked up the yellow plaid bow on her work flats.

With butterflies winging through her chest, she headed out of her office.

She waited at his door, which was already open. He proved to be in deep thought, poring over his computer and some notes on his desk. And, damn, he looked gorgeous all thoughtful, strong and silent. She stood for a moment, watching, enjoying the view. Slowly his gaze drifted from the computer to the doorway.

"Knock, knock," she said.

His face brightened, and he stood. "Hi. Come on in."

The genuine welcome made a little happy spot crop up in her chest, until he schooled his expression to all-business mode, making her doubt he was happy to see her. Mitchell looked handsome, as always. His hair was mussed, with one lock dangling over his forehead, and she had the urge to run her fingers through it in the guise of fixing it, but practiced restraint.

"Have a seat. Can I get you some water or coffee?" It sounded more like obligation.

"Oh, no, thanks." She took a chair opposite his desk, wondering why he'd gone from warm to chilly as he sat down again. *May as well get right down to business, then.* "Say, have you gotten any calls from the local press about Davy Cumberbatch?"

"Nope. Have you?" He discovered and fixed his errant lock of hair with a quick raking of fingers, and she felt she'd fallen off the job by not doing it for him. Silly thoughts, really, but, still, they kept cropping up. Of course she had no right to touch him since they were merely colleagues, though adventurous pod people would always look out for each other. Damn, now he'd gotten her thinking like that again.

The quick memory of their one evening together and the fantasy of touching his hair converged and gave her a little thrill. She forced both thoughts out of her mind and herself back on topic.

"Just dodged a few questions from someone saying they were a journalist from *Talking London*," she continued.

"That rag? Nothing but a gossip paper." He pushed back from his desk. It made the muscles tighten around his upper arms beneath his white polo-style shirt. She shouldn't have noticed but… "You didn't give them any information, did you?"

"No, of course not, but I wonder how they got my personal office number?"

"They're devious, those guys."

"It was a woman, actually."

"Well, be careful. They hound us a lot as we do cosmetic surgery on the rich, royal and famous. Should have warned you about it. Davy Cumberbatch is a biggie over here."

"I suppose they've run out of stories to print about his barroom brawl," she said. "Shown all the gruesome pictures. Now they want the lowdown on how we intend to fix him."

"Guy got his face mangled in that fight, didn't he? Half of it was caved in." He laced his fingers and put his hands behind his head. Did he have a clue how distracting these poses were? "What he expects us to do is going to take a miracle."

"I thought that was our specialty here at Hunter, to make miracles happen. Every day." She quoted the clinic pamphlet. Rather than stare at him, her gaze drifted around his office as she'd never been in it before. He had a striking modern art painting on one wall—she hadn't a clue what it depicted—his diplomas and awards on another, but his solid oak desk was reserved for one single picture frame. It faced him, and Grace wanted more than anything to turn it around and find out who he valued most in life—who got center stage on his desk.

She hoped it was a dog, not a woman. She could deal with him loving his pet.

"Miracles are one thing but rebuilding a face to look like Elvis is a whole different ballgame," he said, still all business.

A light laugh escaped her mouth. Mitch had a knack for putting things in perspective. "I thought he only wanted Elvis's chin, nose and cheeks. And he wanted you to give him Mick Jagger's lips." She considered calling him "Lips" like a few other guys in the clinic, but thought better of it.

"Talked him out of that one. He's down for the whole Elvis package now." Mitchell began to warm up to her, breaking a smile and softening the tension around his eyes. Maybe it was the topic.

"Wise decision. So when do I meet him?" She crossed her leg and laced her hands around one knee.

"He's currently in rehab. That was the stipulation the Hunter Clinic had before we'd take him on as a client. He has to dry out first."

"Another good call." She bobbed her head in agreement.

"Should be out next week." Mitch consulted something on his cell phone. "Yes. Here we go. Next Monday seven p.m. we'll have our consultation meeting."

"Having a meeting after hours won't necessarily keep the paparazzi off his trail."

"True, but they don't have to find out why he's coming here."

"Won't it be obvious?"

Mitch made a mischievous expression, the first she'd seen since the night in the pod at the Eye, or maybe it had been in that elevator at the restaurant, nailing her with his playful green eyes. She'd missed that expression more than she cared to admit. "You don't know about our room, do you?"

"Room? What room?"

"Our ophthalmology room." He used air quotes around *ophthalmology*. "That's how we treat famous people without the press catching on and exposing their plans. Do it all the time for royalty…and actresses and ballerinas and…" He grinned and winked, and it almost made her forget to breathe. "We'll bring Davy in following a press release from Lexi about how he's developed a torn retina due to the fight, then we'll have our consult. See how badly he messed up his face and discuss all the options. Send him out with another prepared statement that we performed laser surgery to repair the retinal tear."

She found herself smiling along with him. "So clever."

"The Hunter Clinic has been doing it for years."

"Still, I can't help but think my abilities could be used for better purposes."

Mitch sat straight and still. "Ah, Gracie, you've forgotten our adventurous-pod-people oath."

Finally, he'd brought that up again! Knowing he hadn't forgotten made her glad. But the look she gave him, tossing her gaze toward the ceiling, conveyed she'd reached her limit on pod-people jokes, even though it was nice to have Mitch back on full form. If she hadn't been taken aback by him calling her Gracie, the name her little sister, Hope, had used to call her, she would have used words. *Not that tired joke again. Really, Cooper.*

Well, if he was giving her a nickname, she needed to come up with one of her own for him. She wouldn't dare go for the garish "Lips", but if the one she had in mind was good enough for Leo, it was good enough for her.

"Apparently, *Cooper*, I have forgotten that oath."

She saw a glint of amusement in his deep eyes when she called him Cooper. Yes, he liked that.

"Fix the rich to help the poor." Now, there he went surprising her again. This time with his valor.

"Kind of like Robin Hood?"

Their eyes connected and every thought about work, nicknames, and oaths—no matter how spot on it was—flew out the window behind him. She noticed his five-o'clock shadow and thought how sexy it was, wondered what he looked like first thing in the morning with messed-up hair to match.

"A bit."

She needed a moment to recuperate.

They'd finished their conversation about Davy Cumberbatch. He'd called her Gracie, she'd called him Cooper. He'd reinforced the Hunter Clinic mission statement, which was a new twist on Robin Hood, along with their pod-person oath—young adventurers unite! Their meeting with Davy C. was scheduled for next week. There really was no reason to stick around. *Get up. Do it now or you'll embarrass yourself staring at him too long.*

She stood to leave, shifting her position so she had a better angle to see the photo on his desk. "Well, I'll buckle down on studying The King's face, and come up with the cheek, nose and chin implants before next Tuesday, then." At least that would give her something to do on her second weekend in London. Alone. "I imagine Davy Cumberbatch will want to see what I have in store for him."

Her gaze slid in line with the photograph. It

wasn't a woman. Or even a dog. Yippee, and thank heavens. It was a beautiful little girl.

Unable to stop herself, she smiled and picked up the frame. "Do you mind?" She didn't wait for his okay. "Who's this lovely little princess?"

His eyes lit up with pride. "That's my Mia. My baby girl."

Grace lifted a single eyebrow. "She's not a baby any more, Cooper. I hate to tell you. My gosh, she's sweet looking." A round face with huge eyes smiled happily at her. Loads of light brown hair curled around her head. Mia had the kind of cheeks Grace wanted to pinch. Or kiss.

"You're right about that. She turned five in March. She doesn't like to be treated like a baby anymore either."

She smiled, enjoying his fatherly frustration. "Do you get to see much of her?" He'd told her he was divorced, which meant he probably had to share time between his ex with his visitation days and all.

He looked confused. "Uh, every day."

"She lives with you, then?"

He'd gone back to shuffling papers around his desk. "Yes, I've got her full-time."

"Oh." What was she supposed to make of that? He was divorced, not a widower, so why would he have full custody of his child? "So she's already acting all grown-up, huh?"

He lifted his brows in agreement, passed a quick glance to the ceiling. "Drives me and the nanny crazy, too."

Since things weren't adding up the way she'd expected, she may as well take advantage of the opportunity to find out as much as possible about him and his living situation. "What's your nanny's name?"

"Roberta. She's a regular Mrs. Doubtfire, and thinks Mia is the granddaughter she never had… which would be impossible because she never had a child herself."

Grace wanted to pump her fist in the air with this new bit of information. There wasn't another woman in Mitchell's life—his ex-wife was completely out of the picture—just an adorable kindergartner plus a plump, middle-aged nanny—that was, if she truly was a Mrs. Doubt-fire type.

Still, the news buoyed her spirit more than she had expected. She smiled at Mitch and put the picture frame back on his desk, not wanting to make too big a deal about it, though she had a thousand other questions spinning around in her mind she'd like to ask like, *how long have you been divorced? Who left whom? Why are you the one with full custody?*

She leaned on her knuckles, edging forward as if he were a giant magnet and she a helpless piece of metal. They smiled playfully at each other.

He glanced at her mouth, and Julie Treadwell's recent surgery came to mind. There really was something about that mouth that seemed so familiar. Grace pressed her lips together, suddenly bashful about them and wondering why Mitch kept staring in that vicinity on her face. He got an I'm-a-naughty-boy flash in his eyes, as if he knew that she suspected what he'd done, and he didn't care! Was it her mouth? The thought, coupled with his flashing eyes, gave her a bout of tingles.

Thankfully the scarf she wore covered her chest under the thin white silk fabric. Their subtle moment stretched on and Grace felt the tips of her breasts tighten. She'd have to be the first to look away, any second now…before she embarrassed herself.

Too late.

Colleague. Colleague. Colleague. All business. Business. Business. Adventurous pod people no more.

"Okay, then, I'll leave you to your work." She should have cleared her throat first, she sounded way too husky for five in the afternoon. She stood straight, leaving his desk behind. "I'll study up on rocker Davy's face, see if he has what it takes to become The King."

"Don't worry, we'll make him a hunk-a-hunk of burning love." Why did he always resort to humor when things got heavy? She glanced back at him, pretending his joke had landed on deaf ears. "We're a great team, you know."

Were they a great team? Gracie and Cooper? Could she bear working with him all the time, having to keep that safe distance when desiring so much more?

"Nice scarf, by the way," he called after her, when she made it through the door.

She left his office smiling, but the spell was short-lived. There were so many mixed messages from Cooper, none of which she could ever possibly follow through on, and everything made her head spin.

What did it matter if Mitch was free, she could only dream about being with someone like him since she'd never, ever, let anyone close again. She couldn't bear to see the shock or pity on any man's face once they saw her scars. Once had been enough. Never again.

She walked back to her office and plopped behind her desk with one thought she simply couldn't let go of. Where was Mitch's ex-wife? He'd said he was divorced the first night they'd met. The wife wasn't dead. Now she'd seen his beautiful child, Mia. The pressing question was, why any woman in her right mind would let a man like Mitch and a daughter like Mia go?

* * *

Mitch stared at the door where Grace had stood. He inhaled the lingering fruity, refreshing scent she always wore. The fragrance did crazy things to his thinking and libido and took him off in all the wrong directions.

He'd done a miserable job of keeping her at arm's length just now.

Gracie. Really, Cooper?

Without trying, they'd moved on to the nickname stage. He was grateful she hadn't chosen Lips. Giving nicknames was something friends did, and they couldn't be friends. Not with the feelings she stirred up inside him just by sitting across from him.

They couldn't be lovers because they worked together and he'd learned from his mistakes, plus he couldn't put things out of balance for Mia. He'd given up gorgeous women, had put his superficial side on hold for good. Mia had been through enough at such an early age, and she deserved a stable, normal mommy.

But he couldn't get the image of Grace leaning across his desk out of his mind. He had to imagine her cleavage, though. Why did she always keep herself covered from neck to knees? She was blessed with a beautiful body—he'd seen the curves—so why did she work so hard to hide everything? He hadn't seen those beautiful legs again since her first day on the job.

Plus all the extra clothes she wore made it harder to imagine her naked…still, he had, just that morning in the shower.

Mitch ran both hands through his hair. What the hell was he supposed to do about Gracie?

Mitchell got the memo about the 8:00 a.m. Friday morning meeting in Leo's office just after Grace had left on Thursday afternoon. The blip on his computer helped him stop thinking about her— not to mention thinking about her naked—and the meeting memo also ended his brief enjoyment over teasing her. Against his better judgement, it was something he'd quickly become fond of in the short time she'd been at the clinic—teasing Grace. And it had to stop. He'd have to go against all his natural instincts where she was concerned, and continue to keep that arm's length between them. He'd made sure to avoid her the last several days. He hated the thought, but knew it was imperative if they were to continue working together.

Upon his arrival at the clinic on Friday morning, he went directly to the meeting. Across from Leo's desk sat the large and quiet Ethan. Though the younger of the brothers, Ethan's life experience, including his injuries, had made him look like the older of the two. It was no secret around the place that the brothers had issues still simmering between them. Sometimes their strained relationship made Mitchell feel uncomfortable.

"Ah, Cooper, I'm glad you're here," Leo said as Mitchell took a seat next to Ethan. Mitchell and Ethan nodded at each other but didn't shake hands, then Mitchell greeted Leo with a smile. "Coffee?" Leo offered a stainless-steel canister.

"No, thanks. Already had mine," Mitchell said. Tension crept up his spine regarding the meaning of this meeting, and he wasn't sure how to read Ethan's withdrawn body language today. Had he done something wrong? Ethan drank from a mug and in between swallows seemed to be pondering something floating inside the coffee cup, reticent as always.

"Well," Leo said, "I wanted to bring you both up to date about some future plans. As you know, our clinic wants to support Fair Go, the charity Olivia Fairchild—a pediatric plastics nurse who used to work here—has started in Africa." Leo poured himself more coffee. "In order to help as many children as possible, I've decided to bring Olivia over for a period of time. I don't know how long it will end up being, actually." Leo looked cautiously at Ethan, and Mitchell also glanced at him, noticing Ethan's grip tighten around the coffee mug. "Until we can afford to eventually go as a team to Africa, we'll have to bring the children here. And she's got a special case she'd like to start with. Unfortunately, she can't adjust her schedule just now." Ethan glanced up. Leo nailed him with a stern look. "So you may as well get used to the fact that one way or the other you'll be working with her, Ethan."

Ethan put his mug down and stood. "Fine with me." He turned and headed for the door but stopped there. He stared at the floor. "Do whatever you have to do. The kids need our help. They come first. Count me in." Then he left. Leo cleared his throat and glanced at Mitchell, who was trying to figure out why working with this doctor should be a concern to Ethan.

"Look, you deserve an explanation, but it's a long, long story," Leo said, as if reading Mitchell's mind.

Mitchell understood Ethan had been through a lot, and could be described as moody at times, but he'd never been rude or obstinate with him. He'd always been professional and Mitchell could see how much he cared about his patients. Mitchell had nothing but respect for him, felt he was a top-notch surgeon. Leo, on the other hand, had seemed to suffer the brunt of Ethan's demons since his return to the family clinic. Mitchell had also overheard many heated arguments behind closed doors since his arrival at Hunter Clinic, and took that into account.

Leo took a drink of his coffee, tension pressing down his brows. "It's a long story, but the basic fact is there's some history between us and Olivia." Leo took another drink. Mitchell understood that the Hunter brothers were limping along and trying to mend their relationship. What Leo meant by "history" between the three of them gave Mitchell pause. Could it mean what he thought? If so, that gave a whole new meaning to family feud.

"Maybe I will have some coffee," he said, and Leo poured him a cup. He took a long warm draw on the rich drink, and waited for the rest of the story.

"I'm sure you know that Ethan will do anything as far as humanitarian efforts go, so, like he said, I know he's on board with whatever Olivia wants to do, whenever she wants to do it. Fair Go is a great organization. I have my suspicions about what may be eating at him, but it's not for me to say." Leo took another drink.

Mitch wanted to be respectful of the brothers and their issues. He also knew Leo well enough that if he wanted to share the full story, he would. He drank his coffee and kept quiet.

"There's one more thing." Mitchell looked up. Was he about to hear the big secret? "And this is just between the two of us." Mitchell gave his nod of confidentiality. *Finally, after being here four years, he's opening up to me. I feel like this is taking our business friendship to a new level.* "Whether my brother wants to admit it or not, he's got a heart." Leo rubbed his eye with the palm of his hand, tried to smile but failed miserably. "If you think he's in a bad place now, just wait until Olivia arrives. I suspect her return will be tough on him, so if you think he's moody now, this is just a warning."

Mitchell put his cup on Leo's desk and stood. "I'll take that on advisement, and won't take any fallout personally." He reached across the desk and shook Leo's hand.

He wanted to thank him for filling him in, but the fact was Leo hadn't disclosed anything. He was a private man, and Mitchell shouldn't have expected him to open up to him beyond the bare essentials. Ethan would be forced to deal with a woman from his past, and Leo had simply wanted to warn him about it. Obviously, something major had happened between the Hunter brothers and this Olivia person, but what it was Mitchell couldn't fathom a guess.

The Hunter Clinic did great work on many levels, yet where the personnel's private lives were concerned, well, emotionally the place was the pits.

"Oh, and Cooper? We've got an explosion survivor on his way over from Ethiopia. One of Olivia's Fair Go children. Lost part of his face and an ear. His name is Telaye Derege. As I mentioned earlier, Olivia can't rearrange her schedule to be here just yet, so I'm assigning you and Grace to him." He tossed a pile of papers at Mitchell. "Here are the case notes. Take them home and study them over the weekend. You two can tackle the boy after the Cumberbatch case. It'll probably take that long for clearance of all the travel documents."

Mitchell picked up the notes, wondering how in the hell he was supposed to keep Grace at arm's length if they kept being assigned the same cases.

He left Leo with more questions formed than answered, and returned to his office.

Just before he entered, he saw Lizzie round the corner. He silently flagged her down and waved her into his office. If anyone knew the whole story, being the new Mrs. Hunter, she would. He waited inside his office until Lizzie joined him then closed the door.

"I've got a question for you."

"Sure. What do you want to know?" she said.

"I've just come from a meeting with Leo, and I'm trying to figure something out."

"Really. What has Leo done now?" She smiled with the understanding look of a woman deeply in love.

"Well, we all know about Fair Go and how we want to give the organization our support."

She nodded, her carefully shaped brows arched earnestly.

"But I've just been informed that Olivia Fairchild herself will be coming to the clinic. When Ethan heard that, he got up and left the meeting, as if she was the last person on earth he wanted to see. And Leo said something about it being a long story and there was some history between the three of them. Then he warned me that Ethan might be a bear to work with once she arrives. What the heck am I supposed to make of that?"

By the expression on her face, Lizzie seemed

to know exactly what Mitchell was referring to. "I don't want to break Leo's trust, but I know how much he respects you as a colleague and a friend. He's not very good at opening up, and I can see why you're confused." She touched his arm. "I know I can trust you, Mitchell, and you deserve to understand why Ethan might be tough to work with for a while, so I'm going to tell you what the issue is."

She perched on the edge of the chair across from his desk. He leaned against the desk, legs outstretched and arms folded. "The short and sweet version is that the 'history' Leo's talking about is a love triangle."

Mitchell drew in his chin then shook his head. Brothers? "What?"

"Both Leo and Ethan had a thing for Olivia a long time ago. Ethan won, then just as quickly broke Olivia's heart. Having spent time with Ethan when he was recuperating, I know he still carries a great deal of pain and guilt from his time in combat, and there were people he cared deeply about and lost during his tour of duty. I suspect having Olivia here at the clinic will force him to remember some things he may want to forget, and he may have to face the fact that he once really cared for her. It's not my place to say anything more, but I hope that helps a little."

"Yes. Thank you. I don't want to delve into places I don't belong, but you've given me more angles to consider."

"Anytime, Mitchell."

"Oh, and Lizzie, how are those honeymoon plans going?"

Her soft brown eyes nearly twinkled at the mention of her delayed honeymoon. "Fantastic. Never in my dreams did I ever think I'd have a wedding like that, and now the most incredible honeymoon. I won't bore you with all the details, but it will be unforgettable, I'm sure of it."

"That's great. Just great. I'm looking forward to hearing all about it when you get back."

She smiled. "Believe me, I'll be telling everyone about it." She paused and a tiny smile crossed her mouth. "Well, not everything."

With that she left Mitchell to his thoughts. A love triangle? Holy smoke, never in a million years would he have come up with that. It was true that women found Ethan mysterious, and from the ladies' scuttlebutt around the water cooler at the clinic, sexy as hell. Leo was also a fantastically handsome guy, not that Mitchell normally noticed such things but in Leo's case it couldn't be denied. Mitchell had always gotten the idea that Ethan was more of a love-'em-and-leave-'em guy. That Olivia must be some woman to have gotten under his skin.

With his interest piqued about what to expect from Olivia Fairchild, he went over what else Lizzie had told him. Olivia would bring back memories Ethan probably wanted to forget about from his time in combat. Mitchell could only guess what he'd been through.

And he thought he'd had it bad. He shook his head, thought about the woman he'd lost bit by bit through plastic surgery, his ex-wife. He'd stuck by her even through her transformation, only then learning she'd fallen in love with his business partner back in California, the only man Mitchell had allowed to do all her surgeries. The two people he'd trusted most had stabbed him in the back and run off together. The rush of memories turned the rich coffee he'd just shared with Leo bitter as ashes in his stomach.

CHAPTER FOUR

ALEXIA ROBBINS KNEW how to be persistent, and Grace was feeling the full force of her won't-take-no-for-an-answer attitude.

Friday afternoon, Grace had just gotten back from the Lighthouse, having assisted on a pediatric cleft palate and extreme nose deformation case with Ethan. Besides being highly impressed with his surgical skills, she noticed how meticulous he was on every level. His team was kept on their toes at all times as he was a man willing to think outside the box when it came to solutions. He'd probably gotten that skill set from his years in combat in mobile surgical units.

The surgery had gone on far longer than she'd expected. She was tired and all she wanted to do was finish her paperwork and head for home to take a nice long bath. But there stood Lexi before her desk, determination flashing in her bright blue eyes and with notepad in hand.

"You've been dodging me, Miss Turner." Lexi put her hands on her hips in mock anger.

"*Moi*? I've been in surgery all day."

"I'm talking about yesterday, and the day before that."

"Surgery and surgery. I'm sorry." Truth was, she *had* been avoiding Lexi and her interview request almost as much as she'd avoided Mitch because of his irresistible charm.

"It's just a few questions. I do it with all our new staff."

Lexi wore the most fashionable clothes, and today was no exception. Her short dress fit to a tee, accenting her curves, and the flashy blue-and-bright-green pattern drew out the color of her eyes. What Grace would give to wear an alluring neckline like that....

"Our clients expect to know all about you."

That would never happen! Grace's mind raced for ways to answer her questions without really revealing anything. "Okay. Shoot." *As in you may as well shoot me because I hate interviews!*

"Lovely." Lexi sat in the white leather chair across from Grace's modern glass and wrought-iron desk.

"I'll answer your questions if you'll answer a few of mine—deal?"

Lexi didn't need long to think about the offer. "Deal. Now, firstly, what is your educational background?"

Grace ran down the list of her universities and medical schools, skipping the part about having to take a year off to recover, then all her awards and certificates.

"Ever married? Any children?"

"Never married. No children. Though I was engaged once," Grace said, without thinking. She hadn't thought about Ben in ages. Even now, after all these years, the thought of him twisted her stomach into a knot. "Once upon a time."

Lexi lifted the thick-lashed lids of her dazzling blue eyes, made up to perfection, gauging the meaning of her response. "Care to elaborate?"

The fact that the guy couldn't accept her after she'd been burned? Hell, no. There would be no elaborating. "Not really."

"I understand."

Could anyone understand? Grace had been through a half dozen skin grafts, she'd finally been given the okay to get up close and personal with her fiancé again, but he'd taken one look at her naked—her breasts and neck covered in webbed and mottled scars—and, as hard as he'd tried, hadn't been able to hide his horror.

"Pets?"

"Pardon? Oh, none. Look, I'm afraid I'm really boring, and people may worry about my stability if we continue." Grace tried to make light of her situation.

"Oh, don't think a second about it. It's hard to pick up and move to London from Arizona. Besides, we're just getting to the good part."

Grace chewed her bottom lip, letting anxiety overtake her, wishing she'd never agreed to the interview. Moving on from heartrending, what could the "good part" possibly be?

Mitch popped around the corner of her office door, his mouth formed to ask a question. Grace and Lexi stopped and glanced his way.

"Oh, uh, never mind. Just had some news to catch you up on."

"Yes?" She wanted more than anything to hear that news, anything to put off this horrible interview. Next Lexi would be asking to take a picture, the second-most dreadful thing Grace could think of after an interview.

"It can wait," he said, and off he went.

Damn, there was no getting out of the rest of the interview now. How could she concentrate, wondering what his "news" was?

"Have a nice weekend." Lexi quickly settled back into the rhythm of their interview. "Tell me about your most amazing reconstructive surgery experience."

Ah, finally something she could shine about....

She smiled, relaxing into her thoughts, and laced her fingers together over one knee. "When I first began my reconstructive-surgery fellowship, I was fortunate enough to be chosen by my mentor to be on her special surgical-reconstruction team. She was one of seven plastic surgeons, along with several other surgeons, led by another woman doctor, taking part in one of the earliest face transplants in the world. Maybe you heard about it? The whole procedure took twenty-two hours…"

Lexi's eyes widened with interest as she scribbled with all her might on her writing pad, her diamond engagement ring gleaming in the overhead lights.

Grace paced the length of her apartment for a third time on a Friday night. She was too tired to go out to eat, especially by herself, and had settled for canned soup with toast. The soup was warming on the stove and the bread waiting for the toaster. Keyed up from a busy week, especially that day's intricate surgery and Lexi's interview, knowing that next week she'd meet her first high-profile patient, she'd soaked in the tub without relief. Feeling a bit in between things, she was restless yet not tired enough to go to bed. Besides, it was only seven o'clock, and she hadn't eaten her supper yet.

She'd blown her opportunity to turn the tables and get the lowdown on Mitchell from Lexi. Something told her there was quite a story

behind his divorce and unusual custody arrange-
ment. Maybe he'd married someone famous? As
adorable as Mia was, her mother had to be gorgeous. Of course, having such a good-looking
dad as Mitch had a lot to do with it, too.

She sat on the couch and fiddled with the TV
controller, not having a clue what programs or
channels were available on British television, set-
tling on an international news station which was
focusing on Spain at the moment, but, whatever,
the news would act like white noise and she'd
have to make do for now.

Her intercom beeped.

She jumped, never having heard it before. What
was that about?

She crossed the room and pressed the button.
"Yes?"

"Uh, it's Mitch. Have you got a few minutes?"

The sound of his voice sent a platoon of nerves
marching through her. The one thing she'd felt
relaxed about for the weekend was being guar-
anteed she wouldn't have to be near Mitchell
Cooper, wouldn't have to fight her interest, or

the reaction of her body, whenever he was near. Now, it seemed, he'd followed her home.

Since she hadn't been successful at getting him out of her mind, she may as well let him in!

"Mitch? Oh, uh, of course I've got time." The guy had come all the way to her apartment, she couldn't exactly refuse him. "Let me ring you in."

The moment she'd pressed the Open button she made a beeline for the bathroom to brush her hair and check her makeup. There was none there! Oh, my. She snatched her gloss and brightened her lips with a few dabs. Then she headed straight to the closet for a thin teal-green sweater to cover her arms. Shoot, she didn't have a turtleneck on so grabbed the nearest scarf, trying to remember how to tie a simple slipknot. She doubled up the scarf and wrapped it around her neck, then slipped both ends into the loop, with fumbling fingers. The result looked haphazard, but it would have to do.

Just as she finished with the scarf, her doorbell rang. Remembering she'd put on comfortable sweat pants after her bath, she groaned. Cripes! She slipped across the carpet to answer the door, turning off the TV on the way and only then realizing she was barefoot.

Mitch smiled when she opened the door, the vision of his strikingly handsome face taking her aback, as it always did at first glance. He wore an old brown leather bomber jacket over his tailored yellow shirt, brown slacks and loafers. He'd removed his tie and the collar was open at his throat.

Her eyes drifted downward to where he held a tiny girl's hand—the beautiful child from the picture. The sweetest-looking thing she'd ever seen.

"Hello!" she said, all thoughts of how she was dressed disappearing. "You must be Mia."

Mia's eyes lit up. "Hi!"

"Sorry," Mitch said, looking at his daughter. "Should have introduced you first. My apologies, Mia, it wasn't polite of Daddy to forget you."

"That's okay." She sounded so grown up.

While his eyes were in the vicinity of his daughter, and the carpeted floor, Grace realized he'd noticed her bare feet. Besides her hands and face, this was the only "naked" part of her he'd ever seen, and it felt intimate. Really intimate.

A slow, warm trail sprang from the soles of her feet to the backs of her knees and kept heading north. She wanted to turn under her bright pink-tipped toes and rush off to put on some shoes.

The moment stretched on a bit too long, and Grace wished Mia would save the day.

Still looking preoccupied with her feet, Mitch flapped a pile of papers at her. "I'm sorry to invade your Friday night, but I thought you'd like to see these case notes on our next patient as soon as possible."

Our next patient?

"Come in," Grace said, after the initial shock let up a bit. "Come in."

"Nice digs," Mitch said, after taking a quick inventory of the living room.

"What beautiful flowers!" Mia had rushed to the coffee table where the calla lilies remained. The same ones that had welcomed her almost two weeks ago—they looked worse for wear, a little droopy with browning edges. The ones Grace kept meaning to throw out. Yet Mia found them beautiful.

Grace smiled, loving the child's enthusiasm, wishing she could tap into it herself.

"They're called calla lilies, Mia, and I think they're pretty, too." She glanced up and saw a beaming Mitch, looking on with adoring fatherly eyes, and wanted to hug him.

Mia quietly repeated the name of the flowers, "Calla lilies, calla lilies," as if memorizing the new words.

"Oh." Remembering her makeshift dinner, Grace dashed for the kitchen. "Pardon me while I turn off the stove."

The open-style apartment made the kitchen easily viewed from the living room.

"Didn't mean to interrupt your dinner, too. Sorry."

"It's only soup and toast, but I can make grilled cheese sandwiches if you're hungry."

"We've just come from dinner, thanks." He followed her into the glaringly white kitchen.

"I'd like a grilled cheese sandwich!" Mia spoke up, hot on her father's heels.

Mitch looked surprised. "You just had chicken

and salad, honeybee, how can you still be hungry?"

"I'm a growing girl?"

Grace laughed and Mitch reluctantly joined her. She loved the way he called Mia "honeybee". So sweet.

Mia, realizing she'd become the center of their attention, grinned. "That's what you always say, Daddy."

Grace went right into action. "Two grilled cheese sandwiches coming up. Do you like tomato soup, Mia?"

"Yes."

Grace smiled at Mitch, who shrugged.

"Then we'll both have a bowl. Can I offer Daddy a sandwich and some soup, too?"

"Thank you, but no. Unlike my daughter, who left most of her dinner on the plate, I'm full."

Grace went back on task. "You can sit right here, Mia, on this stool." She moved and then assisted the child onto the kitchen stool placing it near the small breakfast bar and the stovetop. "Can you stir this soup for me once in a while so I can make the sandwiches?"

Mia's eyes brightened and she reached for the long wooden spoon. "Yes."

Her voice was sweet and serious and it touched Grace's heart. What a precious child Mitch had.

A dreary dinner alone had taken on a new, welcome and completely enjoyable turn. She'd been kept so busy on the job that she hadn't realized how people-starved she'd been since moving to London. Back home, her Friday nights were often spent eating out with her sister. She really missed having someone to share things with—wished she could talk to Hope about Mitch and her mixed-up feelings about him, too, but the seven-hour difference kept her from picking up the phone and calling home whenever she wanted.

Her smart yet lonely apartment had seemed to come to life since Mitch and Mia had walked in the door.

Mitch watched Grace move about the kitchen with ease. She knew how to fend for herself, and he liked that. He liked the fit of her workout pants and the extra treat of catching her barefoot. She had pretty, slender feet, and the pink toenails were downright sexy.

Mia lit up under Grace's natural warmth and kind indulgences, as she carefully stirred the soup, Grace nearby, making sure she wouldn't burn herself or spill anything. Maybe she had nieces and nephews, and was used to being around kids.

"How'd you find out where I live?" Grace asked.

"I had to bribe our beloved receptionist, Helen."

"Ah. Did she give you my phone number, too?"

She sent a subtle message: call before popping in next time. Truth was he'd been afraid she'd put him off if he called first, and he'd really wanted to see her tonight. All through dinner bits of memories about Grace played out in his mind. Mia had gotten impatient at one point, tapping his hand and saying, "Daddy, Daddy, Daddy, don't forget about me!"

"I, uh, forgot to ask, but that's a good idea. We should exchange phone numbers since we'll be working together so much."

After his meeting with Leo, being told he'd be

working with Grace on Telaye Dereje's case, he'd had a perfect excuse to stop by.

"Makes sense," Grace said. "Remind me before you leave and we can put each other's numbers in our cell phones."

He liked that idea, as he watched Grace grill the sandwiches and Mia stir the soup. Things grew quiet.

"What's your favorite dinner, Mia?" Grace asked out of the blue.

"Ice cream." Mia raised her shoulders and twisted her little body in delight, then mischievously glanced at her father. "Sometimes Daddy lets me have ice cream for dinner."

Grace's eyes, so blue, so beautiful, went wide. "Ice cream." She gave him a you-are-so-busted glance.

"Now, Mia, that was only for your birthday," he said, saving face. He really was a conscientious father and worked hard at the job, and he didn't want Grace thinking he was some kind of flake, spoiling his daughter by giving in to her every whim.

Grace grinned at him, understanding in her

eyes. "I think a birthday is a perfectly acceptable time to have ice cream for dinner." She'd already started to grill the sandwiches and had flipped the first one. "I think I'll have ice cream for my next birthday, too."

"When's that?" He took the opportunity to fill in some of the blanks about Grace Turner, reconstructive surgeon. He looked her up and down. Why was she still wearing a scarf around her neck in her own home yet her feet were bare?

"October. I'll be thirty-three, if you're curious."

"Wow, that's old!" Mia said.

He grimaced and pinched his temples with his finger and thumb, then shaded his eyes. "Now, Mia, I'm much older than that."

"How old?" Grace seemed to jump at the opportunity to find out his age, too, and for some reason that made him glad.

"Thirty-six. Won't be thirty-seven until next January."

Grace gave a deadpan glance at Mia. "Now, that's old." Mia covered her mouth and giggled, and stirred the soup with the other hand.

"Okay, okay, ladies, let's move on."

Grace finished the grilling, ladled out two small bowls of soup and Mitch helped carry the sandwiches to the table.

"Are you sure you don't want anything?" she asked.

"I'm fine. Thanks." Just before sitting down to eat, they had another meaningful glance into each other's eyes, the kind that made time stop while swimming through her pale blue stare. He needed to ground himself or he'd start getting all kinds of bad ideas about what he'd like to do with and to Grace Turner. And though he'd once been drawn to beauty like a moth to flame, he'd given up women like her, finding most of them to be vain and superficial. Not so the case with Gracie, though.

"Mind if I talk about the new case while you eat?" he asked.

She blew over the soup on her spoon before tasting it. "Not at all." Grace seemed far too natural to be vain.

While Mia ate like she hadn't been fed all day, embarrassing him no end, and Grace daintily nibbled her sandwich and sipped her soup, Mitch filled her in. The boy had some kind of blast injuries and was from Ethiopia. Plans were being made to fly him over through Fair Go.

Grace listened intently.

Sitting at a table, like they were a family, clutched him around the chest, forcing him to realize how important it was. How he missed it from his childhood, and had never come close to being a family with Christie.

Was Mia lonely for a family? She certainly shined under Grace's attention. Maybe he should ask her out strictly for Mia's sake?

After they ate, he helped with the dishes, against Grace's protest.

"So, I was thinking," he said, drying the non-stick grill pan, "Mia and I are going to the park on Sunday, would you like to come along? You know, get you out of the apartment and show you some of London. What do you say?" He hadn't felt this nervous asking a woman out since he'd first moved to Hollywood and started noticing A-list models. Especially since it was a woman he'd vowed to keep at arm's length for his own good.

She gave him a surprised expression, then glanced at Mia, who'd started clapping, then she tossed him a not-fair-how-can-I-refuse gaze. "Sure. I don't have any plans and it's supposed to be a beautiful weekend, according to the TV weather report."

"Great. Let's have breakfast out first. How about I pick you up at ten?"

"Uh, okay."

It was a dirty trick—how could she say no in front of his daughter?—but he didn't care. Mia liked her and so did he. Damn it. He wanted to spend more time with Grace, whether it was a good idea or not. Today he'd indulge his weakness for beautiful women. Besides, now he knew where she lived.

Before they left they exchanged phone numbers. Against all better judgment, now that he had her number, he may as well use the information.

Grace closed the door and glanced around her apartment. It was as though someone had dimmed the lights. Things looked duller and her energy level had fizzled since Mitch and Mia had left.

Amazed how much they'd brought into her life, she smiled and went around shutting off the lights.

He was a good man and a good father. Mia was a special child who blossomed under her father's attention. But where was her mother? Not once had Mia said anything about a mother. Most kids shared how Mommy did it this way, or how much they liked the way their mother made them grilled cheese sandwiches, but not a peep about a mother from the darling. How long had Mitch's wife been out of the picture, and did little Mia ever have contact with her? Where was Lexi when she needed to pick her brain?

Grace shook her head. It wasn't up to her to figure everything out, no matter how curious she was. What mattered was how much she liked Mitch and the bright and curious Mia.

Grace's heart swelled with affection for both of them, and it caught her off guard. She might not be able to get involved in their lives as much as she'd like, but she sure as hell could be a friend to Mitch and especially to Mia, who needed a mommy, not a nanny.

* * *

Sunday morning, and Mitch arrived as planned at 10:00 a.m., looking fantastic in jeans and a T-shirt. It fit snug and afforded Grace a view of his flat stomach, broad chest, and an in-the-flesh view of the muscles she'd been admiring on his arms all week. Mia wore denim overalls and her hair was in a curly ponytail, high on the back of her head—obviously Daddy's go-to hairdo.

Grace had thrown on jeans and a gray turtleneck. Thankfully, it was a brisk morning, and she wouldn't have to explain why she'd covered up. Again.

In the past, if someone simply had to know why she dressed the way she did, she'd mention her burns. Expecting to end the subject right there, she'd then notice the tsk-tsk expression on whoever it was, and the look would make her crazy. She'd learned well to keep her scars a secret.

Already, it was important to her never to have Mitch give her that tsk-tsk look, or feel sorry for her in any way. So far he hadn't seemed to catch onto the way she carefully kept herself covered. Thank goodness.

"Are you ready for breakfast, Gracie?" he asked.

"Why, yes, Cooper, I'm starving. How about you, are you hungry, Mia?"

"I'm starving, too!" Grace wasn't sure that Mia knew what the word meant, but Mia had mimicked it perfectly with the exact inflection she must have heard in *her* voice. Besides mimicking, the child liked to clap about things, too. This time, Grace found herself imitating Mia, clapping right along.

"Yay," she said, suddenly more enthusiastic about having breakfast out than she could ever remember in her entire life.

"Great, because I'm taking you to our favorite waffle café, and they serve a lot of food."

"Sounds heavenly."

"By the way, you look beautiful today," he said.

Grace almost tripped in her tracks to his car. "Thanks." How should she handle the compliment? "You don't look half-bad yourself." She'd take the superficial route.

He gave her half a smile, letting her know he was okay with her brushing off his flattery.

Seriously, though, he thought she looked beautiful in her jeans and gray turtleneck? When was the last time a man had told her she looked beautiful, or she'd felt beautiful?

Meanwhile, he looked like a men's magazine-cover model, which distracted Grace from the deep discussion with Mia about her latest favorite animated film, something about balloons and children flying to another land where everything was pink and toys could talk....

Forty-five minutes later, looking down on the largest Belgian waffle she'd ever seen, smothered in sliced bananas, and inhaling the marvelous scent of the bananas and fresh maple syrup imported from Maine, she indulged herself in the first bite. She thought she'd gone to taste heaven. A moan of delight escaped her throat.

"Sounds like you're enjoying that a little too much," Mitch said, an envious glint in his eyes.

"You knew what you were talking about," she said, covering her mouth because she hadn't finished chewing. "This place is great."

"Glad you like it." He hadn't bothered to shave that morning and the stubble, combined with his sincere smile, almost had her moaning again, but for an entirely different reason. "By the way," he interrupted her dreamy thoughts, "I thought we'd do something really fun after this."

Her mouth was filled with a second bite of delicious waffle so all she did was look at him.

"I've been meaning to take Mia on one of those amphibious land/boat tours of London since we got here, and have yet to find the time. I thought today would be perfect."

Mia squirmed in her chair with excitement and did her usual clap.

Grace, with her mouth still full, clapped along. She glanced at Mia, and when Mia gave a wide smile, food and all, Grace did the same.

"Girls, get a hold of yourselves." Mitch played along, acting disgusted but obviously loving Grace coming down to his daughter's level.

Why was hanging out with Mitch and his daughter so much fun?

An hour after breakfast, Grace, Mia and Mitch boarded a bright yellow amphibious boat, along with a load of other people. They scrambled to sit toward the front, Mia carefully placed between them. Grace couldn't help feeling like they were a family, and she let herself pretend for a few seconds that they all belonged to each other. It felt too wonderful and scared her. *Don't daydream like this. It will only hurt later.*

"Why are you quiet?" Mia asked.

Grace snapped out of her mixed-up feelings, jumping right back into the here and now. "I'm so excited about this adventure, I needed a moment to say thank you."

"Who did you thank?"

Mia's direct questions forced Grace to think. She gave it a second then smiled at Mitch. "I guess I should say it out loud, then, shouldn't I? Thank you, Mitch, for inviting me along today."

The corners of his eyes crinkled as he smiled, those sea-green eyes piercing right to her center. "I'm really glad you came."

Mia clapped. Grace's good mood swelled with the child's natural enthusiasm.

For the next hour and a half they rode by the usual London tourist sites—Buckingham Palace, Westminster Abbey, Big Ben, Trafalgar Square— and finished up by splashing the big barge-type boat, that was first used in World War II on the beaches of Normandy, into the Thames for an up-close look at the Houses of Parliament.

Mia clapped and squealed as they launched into the water, and Grace laughed along with Mitch. The driver had taken on a ridiculous personality during the trip, Drake McDuck, making everyone laugh and carry on like they were kids again. Forcing them all to say "quack-quack" any time he mentioned his name, which was constantly! Grace couldn't remember when she'd last had so much fun. Then her mind jumped back to two weeks ago and the night she'd first met Mitch, when he'd taken her to the adventure playground.

The thought of having someone like Mitch in her life both scared and appealed to her. But having someone meant opening up and she couldn't do it. Not that he was asking anyway.

A distant amphibious boat created a wake that rocked and rolled theirs. Mitch enjoyed watching Grace's eyes open wide, just like his daughter's. He laughed when Grace and Mia squealed in unison and grabbed hands. Mia was usually shy and withdrawn around grown-ups, but not with Grace. They'd taken to each other right off, as if they'd known each other for years. Seeing how Grace genuinely enjoyed his daughter's company touched his heart. She wasn't faking it, everything about her was real.

When had he felt so lighthearted, so free of burdens lately? He couldn't remember, but looking into Grace's crystal-blue eyes, how they shone with joy against her creamy skin and dark hair, he wanted to grab her and kiss her.

But he knew better. He wouldn't ruin it for Mia. She'd made a new grown-up friend.

After the tour, they grabbed some vendor snacks and walked down to the Jubilee playground again. In broad daylight it was filled to overflowing with children and parents, and the noise level made it hard to talk without yelling. He'd liked it better the night they'd had the place to themselves.

Grace smiled at him. A lot. From across the playground while she pushed Mia on a swing. From the monkey bars as she stood beneath Mia, ready to catch her if she fell. And crawling along behind Mia in a long cylinder replicating a hollow tree trunk, her face lit up the day like the sun could never do.

A tight and sudden clutch in his chest brought him to his senses. It was so apparent how much Mia needed a mother, how she shone under Grace's attention. Every child needed a mother, yet it was the one thing he couldn't give his daughter. It wasn't Grace's job to fill in the blanks in his life. He'd fouled everything up by getting swept away by Christie's beauty. He'd been naive when he'd first opened his medical practice with Rick, his best friend from medical school in Southern California. He'd fraternized with the Hollywood crowd, simply because he'd been able to. Sure, he'd gone into plastic surgery to make big bucks, taking into account that Hollywood and glamour went hand in hand. Suddenly, he and his partner had been the big deal in town, and he'd been seduced by beauty everywhere, the kind of beauty he could make with his own hands.

There was an old saying about Hollywood stealing a person's soul, and for the five years he'd had his practice there, he'd lost his. He'd left the family life and values of his youth behind to explore the superficial and vain side of things. The prettier the women had been that he'd dated, the happier he'd been…or so he'd thought.

Until he'd chosen the most beautiful woman of all, having been completely captivated by her looks, and somehow not seeing past the perfect facade to notice something much greater had been missing. Once they'd married he'd tried to go back to the way things had been when he'd grown up. Marriage meant a family with children. But that approach had proved to be a disaster. And his precious Mia had suffered the cruelest of all costs—a detached mother.

He shook his head and focused back on Grace, currently running and laughing with Mia. She was a busy surgeon, in a new city, probably just getting her bearings. It wasn't fair to expect anything from her. It wasn't safe either. What if Mia got too attached to Grace?

She was a business colleague, and that should be all. He'd have to pay for his mistakes and poor choice of a business and personal partner by himself.

An anxious reflex drilled through him. Had he made a mistake, asking Grace out today?

"Can we go to the pagoda?" Mia rushed him, catching him off guard. The Chinese Pagoda in Kew Gardens was, for some reason, his daughter's favorite place.

"It's getting kind of late, honeybee."

She used her surefire approach and jumped up and down, while saying, "Please, please, please?"

"I'd love to see Kew Gardens," Grace said. "That is, if it isn't cutting too much into your plans for the rest of the day?"

Mia clapped.

"On one condition, Gracie."

She stood there looking lovely and sun-kissed from a highly cooperative London day. It was all he could do not to reach out and hug her. "What's that?"

"We stop for some Chinese takeout and have a picnic while we're there."

"I'd love to."

Mia cheered. "Yay, we're going to the pagoda."

* * *

Later, Grace thanked Mitchell for a perfectly lovely day, when he saw her to the front of her building. Mia had fallen asleep, and rather than leave her in the car he hoisted her into his arms. So zonked was she from their long day spent entirely outdoors, that the child rested her head on his shoulder and he carried her as naturally as any father worth his salt.

He smiled and mouthed, "You're welcome," not wanting to wake Mia.

Somewhere around the time of the playground, he'd changed. His mood had shifted and since then he'd seemed cautious, withdrawn even.

Had she done something to offend him? Maybe she'd pushed it by agreeing to go to Kew Gardens with them, when it was clear he was ready to call it a day. She wanted to ask what she'd done, but it wouldn't be fair to grill a guy with his daughter like a sack of potatoes on his chest and shoulder.

She'd let her hair down and enjoyed every minute of their outing, something she hadn't done with a man since she'd been burned. Mia was such a fun child, she rarely fussed, and she actually listened to reason. He'd done a great job of not spoiling her but making sure she knew she was loved, and Grace wanted to tell him so, but, again, now just wasn't the time.

Sometimes actions spoke louder than words ever could. The man had gone out of his way to show her a good time, and she appreciated it with all her heart.

Too bad he was holding his sleeping daughter. She went up on tiptoe, anchored herself by balancing her hand on his free arm and kissed his cheek.

"I'll always love London because of the way you shared it with me," she whispered.

He looked baffled, as if he couldn't think of a proper reply.

She laughed quietly and shook her head. Men were funny that way. She'd been too honest, and scared him off. Oh, well, at least he knew how she felt.

"I'll see you at work tomorrow," she said, then opened the door to her building without giving him another glance. "Tell Mia good-night for me."

"Will do. Say good-night, Gracie."

She grinned. "Good night, Gracie."

When she closed the door, she leaned her back against it, fighting off the strong desire to know Mitch and his beautiful child more. But one other thing inched into her thoughts—could the reason he blew hot and cold around her be because of unresolved issues with his ex-wife? What if he still loved her?

Then why was he in one part of the world and she in another? Hell, she had proved to be a lousy snoop. She'd spent the whole day with the man and didn't even know if his ex lived in London or the States.

She sighed—even if there weren't any concerns hanging things up on his end, there could still never be a possibility of them becoming close because of her issues—then she pushed off from the door and headed for the elevator. That about summed up the sorry state of her life—seeing wonderful relationships, longing to have one for herself, but knowing she never could. And she was really getting sick of it.

Damn Mitch for rubbing it in her face.

CHAPTER FIVE

MID-MONDAY MORNING, Mitchell barreled into Grace's office in the clinic with knit brows, looking frustrated. Fired up, as her daddy used to say. Even while obviously testy, she found him appealing. She quashed the thought, switching to all business, as she'd promised herself to do last night, lying in bed, staring at the ceiling, unable to sleep. Thanks to spending the entire day with him!

"I can't believe the hacks out there," he said, stance wide, hands on hips, scrubs fitting deliciously.

"Out where?"

"Do you know what I spent my morning doing?" The O.R. cap brought out that extra bit of blue in his otherwise green eyes, making him even more devastatingly appealing.

"What?"

"Fixing a botched plastic surgery job on a twenty-two-year-old, that's what." He paced the small space in front of her desk. "The guy mangled her lips, making her look like a duck. She had a smile like the Joker from that movie. Grotesque. And why would a surgeon agree to do a face-lift on someone just out of their teens? I tell you, sometimes I don't get our profession."

She considered his anger, threw in some of her own, then thought about their jobs and the oaths they'd taken when they'd become doctors—do no harm. She also thought about something that had been weighing on her mind since she'd been assigned a certain high-profile case.

"Isn't that what we do? Whatever people want? Not the duck-lips part, or the botching-up part, but don't we agree to do whatever our rich patients want? Isn't that what we promised to do for Davy Cumberbatch?"

"This girl is neither rich nor demanding. She's naive, and that hack took advantage of her wanting to look beautiful."

But Grace's direct comments stopped his thunder for a couple of seconds. He stopped pacing and pulled in his chin, as if he hadn't considered the comparison of Hunter Clinic to hacks ever before.

"You said it yourself," she said. "Fix the rich to help the poor? Or something along those lines." She didn't back down.

Maybe she didn't want to let him off the hook because she was still upset with him for tilting her world sideways, for making her see what she could never have. A family. A love of her life. It wasn't in the cards for her, and the Sunday outing with Mitch and Mia had driven that point home. Yes, she was upset with him for making it so clear, and right now she'd make him squirm on a professional level as penance.

"What we do," he said, stepping closer to her desk, balancing on his hands and leaning in, "is completely different from that. Sure, we try to keep the wealthy looking fresh and young as long as possible, but we don't mangle their faces in the process. We give people what they want without making them caricatures of themselves. We know where to draw the line. This guy was a hack. He took this young woman's hard-earned money and botched the job on her face. It took me twice as long to fix his mess as I'm sure it did for him to throw in those lip implants. How can he live with himself?"

She remembered the first case she'd ever scrubbed in on in plastic surgery, how nervous she'd been that she might ruin someone's appearance for life. Her own scars could at least be covered, but what could a person do when their face was ruined? Like the lady who'd had her face nearly ripped off by her pet dogs, and who'd needed a face transplant. She sometimes wondered why people took the chance with cosmetic surgery, but understood there were hundreds of reasons. The business of beautifying people was thriving, and that wouldn't likely change in the future. It was merely a sign of the times.

"Do you ever wonder what makes a woman of her age seek plastic surgery?" she asked.

His frustrated expression turned stone cold. "I've been trying to figure out why women flock to it for years."

"And men."

He nodded his agreement. "Haven't come close to an answer yet."

The fire returned to his eyes, and she found him sexier than ever, leaning over her desk, engaging her in a philosophical discussion on the pros and cons of cosmetic surgery, lip jobs and hacks. She had the urge to grab his tie, pull him close, and kiss him silly.

But she didn't.

Then she noticed he was studying her lips again, and she had a crazy idea. What if he'd "fixed" the botched-up lip job to look like hers? Now she'd gone off at the deep end, imagining things she wanted to believe. That Julie Treadwell mouth repair may have looked similar to her lips, but the rest, him doing it on purpose, was all a crazy fantasy she'd made up. She shouldn't flatter herself like that. Didn't deserve it. But maybe later she could visit Julie and check out her theory anyway.

"As far as Davy Cumberbatch goes, I see your point." Mitch had simmered down on the anger scale, but something else smoldered in his eyes.

"Not many people would call me on it, though. So thanks for pointing it out."

How many men, surgeons no less, ever admitted they were wrong? She really could fall for this guy if she wasn't careful.

"By the way, you look really beautiful again today." Out of the blue he'd focused on her appearance.

"Now you're just buttering me up. What favor do you want?"

Didn't he get it? Once he saw her hidden scars he'd change his mind about her in no time flat. That's how it had been with her ex, and it would be the same with Mitch.

"I'm serious." He engaged with her eyes until she thought she might squirm in her chair, but suddenly he snapped out of it. "When Lucy Grant comes out of Recovery, I'm going to give her a stern talking to. Her face was good enough just the way it was. Now that she has more realistic-looking lips, I hope she doesn't use this face-lift, lip-job experience as an entry-level drug, so to speak."

Back in her residency, Grace had read several

psychology journal articles on people becoming addicted to plastic surgery procedures, and they'd influenced her toward specializing in reconstructive surgery over cosmetic. She figured just about anything in life could become addictive…like gazing into the depths of Mitchell Cooper's eyes.

That frustrated look came back to his face. Something stirred beneath the surface of his thoughts, and the jump in his pulse rate was almost palpable in the air. This case had really gotten under his skin, and she could tell he needed to talk more about it. She wished she had time to be there for him, but her job and patients came first. That was the whole reason she'd come to the Hunter Clinic. "Maybe we can talk later," she said, as she prepared to leave for Kate's. She was due to fix a nasty cheek scar from a car accident on a young woman who was getting ready to head off to college in the states for the summer.

He mumbled something unintelligible in a discontented tone.

For some crazy reason, even that made her smile. He was passionate about his job and had a tendency to wear his emotions on his scrubs. A lovely change from most men she'd known. Bottom line, the guy had way too much influence over her state of mind....

But later never came. When Grace finished the surgery that afternoon and returned to the Hunter Clinic, she stopped by Mitch's office, and he was already gone.

That wouldn't stop her. She wanted to see him. Besides giving him another chance to vent his frustrations, she also had some questions about Davy Cumberbatch and their scheduled meeting tomorrow night.

She wandered out to Helen in the reception area.

"I was looking for Cooper, I mean Mitch. Cooper. Any idea where he is?"

The middle-aged, always-meticulously-coiffed-and-made-up receptionist had a curious twinkle in her gray eyes in response to her question. *I know you're wondering why I should want to know, but it's none of your business. Besides, as his business colleague I have a right to know where he lives. Oh, quit looking at me like that and just tell me already.*

"He had to pick up his daughter early today, as it's the nanny's night off."

How should she go about this? Mitch had gotten her home address out of Gwen, why couldn't she get his out of her, too? Sure, she had his phone number in her cell phone now, she could call him and ask him her questions, but she'd rather talk to him face-to-face. He'd seemed so disturbed about the botched job on the young woman, and they'd barely scratched the surface of the conversation when she'd had to leave.

Not to mention those questions about Davy's consultation.

Truth was she wanted to know where he lived. She wanted to see Mia again, even though she'd talked to herself just last night about not getting too close to either of them. It had only been twenty-four hours and she already missed the child. And Mitch. Besides, today was another day, and she sensed Mitch needed her to bounce his thoughts off.

Wasn't it practically her duty?

And if she went to his house, she preferred to make it a surprise visit, like he'd done—what goes around comes around and all. Being painfully honest, *she* wanted to see *him* look surprised for once.

"Here," Helen said, as she finished scribbling something on a piece of notepaper with the chic Hunter Clinic logo at the top.

Grace pulled out of her thoughts and looked at it—an address, Mitch's address. She hadn't even asked yet. Was she that obvious? "Thank you!"

From the coy Mona Lisa smile on Helen's face, apparently she had been.

Grace stood outside the door of the Marylebone Street house. She liked the quaint appeal of the traditional mews-style home— flat front, two stories, all white except for the front and garage doors, which were a dark and vibrant blue. There were lots of windows to let in daylight, and a huge green vine growing up the beam beside the porch up to the second floor, then branching out and going wild along the second story. A ledge underneath the front window held a long flower box, full to the brim with plants and bright colors. The man seemed to have a green thumb, and overall she was impressed by Mitch's taste.

She hoped he was there, having come all this way in a taxi and already having sent off the driver. Maybe she should have had him wait? In this out-of-the-way London neighborhood, it would be hard to find another cab. But wasn't that what cell phones were for?

Maybe she should have called first. Doubts added up as she cast her glance down the street at the cab growing smaller and smaller. This wasn't the brainiest plan she'd ever hatched, but…

The door swung open, and there stood Mitch in jeans and a green T-shirt, making his eyes look unbearably emerald. His surprised expression soon turned welcoming. "Gracie! I didn't expect to see you again today."

"Well, Cooper, you seemed so irritated earlier I wanted to make sure you didn't come home and take it out on your daughter."

He laughed. "Like that would ever happen."

She knew, without knowing him really well, that he didn't have a mean bone in his body. Especially when it came to his daughter—the guy was a pushover.

"I hadn't even knocked. How'd you know I was here?"

"Saw the cab through the window. Got nosy."

"Okay. Well, anyway, I sort of accused you of being a hypocrite earlier and that wasn't my intention at all," she said, suddenly feeling the need for a full explanation. "I was merely pointing out certain aspects about our jobs that could be examined more."

"It's after hours, Gracie," he said, leaning on the doorframe. "Quit sounding like a professor and come inside."

She flushed, having taken the dry, intellectual route instead of his emotions-on-the-sleeve approach.

"Come on." He motioned her inside. "Mia will be thrilled you're here."

What about you? Are you thrilled I'm here, too? The words were foremost in her mind and on the tip of her tongue as she stepped over the threshold, but she didn't dare utter them. Why did her mixed-up feelings for Mitch make her so damn insecure?

"Have you had dinner yet?" he asked, breaking into her twisted thoughts. "I could throw something together for you." He swaggered down his entryway like a man who knew he was king of his castle. "You know, return the favor."

"I grabbed a sandwich from the buffet at the clinic just before I left. Thanks." The clinic provided just about everything the employees needed, including an exercise pool in the basement and a lounge fully stocked with food.

She glanced around his small but inviting home. It lacked the touch of a woman, with a high technological feel using glass, metal and leather rather than overstuffed cushions and colorful swatches of fabrics. But there was plenty of evidence that a child lived there. One entire corner of the living area was furnished with the latest sturdy plastic playhouse equipment complete with a minitreehouse beside it, big enough for Mia to crawl up into. Wow. Grace had never seen anything like it.

"Gracie!" Mia's usual dainty voice cranked up

in volume when she barreled down the hall and discovered Grace in the living room. "Did you come to see me?"

"Of course I did." Without thinking, Grace bent over and lifted the five-year-old, and swung her round. "I missed you already."

The child's gorgeous smile nearly broke her heart. Mitch stood nearby, a mixture of sex appeal and fatherly pride rolled into one gorgeous package.

An emotional flutter gripped her inside. Maybe it had been a mistake to come here. She'd ignored her better judgement, found an excuse, and insinuated herself right back into their lives. Exactly the opposite of what she'd resolved to do. What the hell was the matter with her?

"Can I get you a drink? Some soda or wine? Tea?"

A bit on edge, she made a snap decision. "You know, a glass of wine doesn't sound half-bad. White, if you have it."

"Coming right up." He was in his socks, and he quietly padded off to the kitchen.

Mia pulled Grace to her play area. "Want to see my house?"

"I sure do. Do you live here all the time?"

That got the reaction she'd hoped for out of the little girl, who giggled. "No. I have a real bedroom. Want to see it?"

"Maybe later, after I'm through visiting with your daddy. But why don't you show me your favorite toy?"

"Okay!" With that Mia ran back down the hall, disappearing behind a door.

Grace took the moment to scan the rest of the living room. Mitch definitely liked modern art as there were several bright splotched paintings decorating his walls, similar to the one in his office. Her gaze zeroed in on a small frame on a smoked-glass table top beside a black leather recliner. In the frame was a photo of a young woman. A beautiful young woman.

Grace's heart sank. Was this his ex-wife? She was a woman worthy of being a famous model or actress. Perfect bone structure like that was rare. She wanted to pick up the picture and study it more closely, but didn't. With a father like Mitch and a gorgeous mother like this—if that's who she was—no wonder Mia was so adorable.

"Here you go," he said, from behind her.

She swung round, startled. "Oh, thanks." She'd been caught staring at the picture, so she may as well fess up. "Is that your ex-wife?" she said, before her filtering process kicked in as she sat down. It was none of her business, why had she asked? But it was too late, she had.

Mitch flattened his lips into a straight line. A resigned expression took over from the earlier welcoming one. He nodded. "Yes."

He'd fallen far short of clarifying why the portrait had been put in such a prominent place, and must have sensed she needed more of an explanation.

"That was taken a couple of years before Mia was born, when we first got married."

"She's lovely, Mitch." Her heart ached to say it, but it was true. Deep-seated insecurities came out of hiding, giving her a defeated and depressed feeling. She tried to hide it. She'd gone from prom queen in high school to nerdy med student in college, and then…the burns, and that progression had shattered her confidence.

After loving a woman as beautiful as this, how could a man settle for a scarred mess like her? Then one more thought popped up, and it hurt even more.

Did he still love his ex-wife? Why else would he leave her picture out?

A distant sad twinge invaded his gaze as he studied the photograph along with her. "Seems like a lifetime ago."

Mia came running back into the room. "Here's Koko, my favorite teddy bear."

"Oh, let me see him. May I hold him?" Grace set down her wine and reached for the black stuffed animal with a red plaid ribbon around its neck, hoping she'd hidden her true reaction to Mitch's unclear explanation about the photograph.

Mia kissed the bear's head and handed him over. Grace rocked him like a baby and poked his stomach while sitting him on her lap, anything to get her mind off that picture. "Aw, he's adorable."

Mia stood close and patted her bear's head gently, like a doting mother. Grace loved the smell of her—fresh children's shampoo mixed with a day of playing. She could have just as easily snuggled with Mia in that chair as the bear.

Satisfied her favorite toy was in good hands, Mia dashed off to play with her other toys in the corner. Mitch sat nearby in a chair exactly like the one she was in, and drank a large glass of water. She took a sip of wine, finding it light and fruity, wishing she was drinking it under different circumstances.

"You're probably wondering why I stopped by," she said.

"You were quite clear about it at the door."

"I'm not being snoopy or anything, I promise. I just got the feeling you needed a little more time to vent about your case today. We were cut short by my schedule."

Half his mouth hitched into a smile. "Ah, yeah, well, I blew that out of my system, thanks to you."

"We're coworkers, and we need to be there for

each other. I feel like I could do the same with you, if I needed to."

"Definitely."

She took another sip of wine then set down the glass. "Mind if I pick your brain a bit about Davy?"

"Not at all. What's up?" Mitch leaned forward in the chair, forearms resting on his thighs, looking upward beneath a creased brow. She could hardly think with those eyes staring her down.

"I don't see how his narrow face can support such high cheekbones. You know—that Elvis look he's after."

Mitch bit his lower lip, and blew out a short breath. "I've been thinking about what you said earlier, about how we were doing the same thing with him as that hack I was griping about today did to my patient."

Oh, she'd touched a sensitive note after all with that observation.

"And you're right. Just because some rich rocker wants to look like Elvis, it doesn't mean we have to help him out. I've decided I'm going to talk to him tomorrow night, see if we can get him to back off a little from that extreme make-over he's looking for."

Grace wished she'd come from home so she could have brought her laptop and the graphic she'd made of how Davy's face would look by overlapping the Elvis features on it. It wasn't a good look on his narrow face. Not at all.

Knowing she'd influenced Mitch into changing his mind about giving in to the guy's every whim made her feel valued and respected—a part of the Hunter Clinic team.

"But if we don't give him what he wants," she said, "what's to stop him from going somewhere else, getting really botched up, and leaving us scrambling to find funds to bring more children to the clinic pro bono?"

Mitch opened his mouth to say something when the beeper hooked over his belt went off. He glanced at the number. "I've got to get this one."

He got up and went in search of his cell phone in the kitchen. She heard muffled talking in the other room and shortly he returned with a torn expression on his face. "Damn, my patient is having some bleeding issues, and I need to go and have a look at her, but I'm in a bind with Mia as Roberta is off tonight."

"You need someone to watch her? I can do that."

"Are you sure?"

"I'd love to, and I don't have any plans tonight other than laundry. That can wait another day."

Relief trickled over his face, changing his worried expression. "I can't thank you enough."

"Don't even think about it."

He went over to Mia, who was busy feeding Koko in the tree house. "Daddy has to go back to work for a little bit, honeybee, but Gracie's going to stay with you. Okay?" He bent and kissed the top of her head.

Mia clapped. "Yay! Bye, Daddy."

"Talk about not feeling needed," he said, half teasing and obviously half insecure.

"I'll take good care of her. Don't worry. I just hope it's nothing serious with that girl."

He pushed his stockinged feet into his loafers and grabbed his keys. "Me, too."

And before she could say another word, he was out the door.

* * *

Mitch rushed home as soon as he was sure Lucy Grant was stable. The butcher job that the first plastic surgeon had done on her had already caused scar tissue to form and he'd had to remove some tissue before he'd put in the new lip implants. The mouth, being rich with vasculature, had bled easily and combined with the fresh surgical swelling had made the evening-shift nurse worry it might be a drug allergy. He did a thorough examination of the surgical site and discovered a leaking vessel, put in one stitch and all was well, but the patient would have extensive bruising and swelling for a couple of weeks.

Almost three hours later, he opened his front door, and headed down the short entryway to discover Grace and Mia asleep in each other's arms. On the sofa, they looked like a sleeping variation on the Madonna-and-child portrait.

Rocked to the core at the sight, he put out his hand and leaned against the wall, just staring at them. He'd made a huge mistake leaving Grace with Mia to bond even more. All his daughter had talked about the rest of Sunday evening had been Gracie, Gracie, Gracie.

This wouldn't do. He couldn't let this go on, yet he'd opened the door and invited her in when Mia had already been under her spell.

He needed his head examined over that decision.

The most disturbing part of all was that he was just as deeply under Grace's spell, only much, much deeper, than Mia.

CHAPTER SIX

MITCHELL REALLY SHOULD wake up Gracie and carry Mia off to bed. Yet he stood there, looking at them from across the room like two parts of a puzzle perfectly fit together on his couch. Grace's long, dark hair feathered across the top of the sofa on one side, and pooled together with his daughter's chaotic brown curls on the other. He took a few steps forward for a better view. A long-forgotten yearning for a complete family prodded his memory. Having given up on that dream ages ago, he pushed it away.

Not gonna happen. The last mommy-material date had bored him to tears.

A guy was supposed to learn from his mistakes. Grace was in a demanding profession and didn't have time for Mia. Twice now he'd seen her go off with Leo to the procedure room for God knew what. For all he knew, she was already well on her way to becoming a plastic surgery junkie, like his ex.

It didn't ring true. She'd been the one to bring up Davy Cumberbatch and cautioning about unnecessary surgeries. And nipping and tucking ad nauseam really didn't seem Grace's style.

A book had fallen from Grace's hand—it rested on one of her thighs. He recognized the cover. *The Tale of Misty Do-Right in the Battle of the Wrongs*. It was his and his daughter's all-time favorite story, a fun way to teach ethics, and had awesome illustrations. Now she'd shared it with Grace. It was a clue how special Grace had quickly become to Mia, and the thought worried him.

Snuggled tightly under Grace's other arm, Mia's head rested on her chest. No doubt his child listened to Grace's slow and steady heartbeat, finding comfort in her sleep. Like mother and child.

The distant ache grew stronger. Mia had missed out on this special kind of closeness with her birth mother...and that was all Christie had turned out to be.

The sight of Grace and Mia entwined like family nearly bowled him over.

He combed fingers through his hair, trying to figure out what to do. Wake them up or enjoy the snapshot in time a moment or two longer? Because if he followed his gut, for the sake of Mia's already broken heart, this couldn't happen again.

He'd let Grace creep under his skin, and as overwhelmingly appealing as she was, especially considering her easygoing relationship with his daughter, he knew it wasn't worth the risk of letting her into his life. It wasn't worth the risk to his heart, or his daughter's. Theirs had both been thrashed by Christie.

It was his responsibility to guard his daughter from ever having her heart broken again. When she grew up, she was sure to get enough of that on her own. For now, at least, he could protect her.

His gaze drifted to the photo of his ex-wife—the woman who was nothing more than a stranger to him now—wondering why he even kept it around. Yet he knew it was for Mia's sake, when she asked about her mommy. Maybe he should put it away. Maybe she'd quit asking and finally forget. Maybe he could prevent the inevitable day when his daughter asked, "Why did Mom leave us, Daddy?"

He had to protect Mia from being hurt and disappointed by a mother figure. Thankfully, the child was too young to remember the devastating blow when Christie had failed to bond with her own baby and made her choice to leave. Both of them.

Grace must have sensed Mitchell's presence, as she stretched and opened one of her eyes. Without a word, in consideration to his daughter, she raised a hand in greeting and mouthed, "Hi," not the least bit self-conscious about being caught asleep in the intimate snoozing embrace.

"Hi," he whispered, moving closer, putting his doctor's bag on the table. "Nice nap?"

She smiled. "Very."

Mia stirred.

Mitch rushed to the couch and picked her up. "I'll put her to bed before she wakes up and gets her second wind. Then w—I'd be up all night." He'd almost slipped and said "we'd".

Grace followed him down the hall and into Mia's room, rushing ahead to pull back the bed-covers in preparation for his girl. What a team.

He was so used to doing everything for Mia himself, it felt as though Grace was invading his territory. Except he kind of liked her helping out, and wasn't that how most parents did things? To-gether? He'd never had the luxury of that. What must it be like?

He watched his daughter hunker down on the mattress, burrowing back into a deep and peace-ful sleep as he tucked the covers beneath her chin.

Grace had tiptoed out already, as if understand-ing he needed this special moment to say good-night to his daughter. *His* daughter. He kissed her forehead lightly, marveling, as he always did, at her preciousness.

Grace deserved an explanation about why he guarded his baby girl so carefully. Maybe one day he'd tell her. What was that old saying—there was no time like the present?

After closing the door except for a crack so the hall light could filter in, as was their habit, he walked back to the living room, thinking how best to approach the subject.

Grace sat on the couch, looking at him expectantly. She seemed to sense his every mood change. "Everything okay? Did she go back to sleep?"

"Like a rock. Thanks." Nervous energy caused his hand to shoot to his scalp again, and though he tried to stop them, his fingers seemed to have a mind of their own, tunneling through his hair.

"I hope you don't mind the messy kitchen, but we baked."

"You baked?"

"Rice Krispies treats. Not really baking, I suppose, but something a five-year-old can help with."

He grinned. He'd left Grace alone with his daughter for two hours and they'd baked together. He should have known she'd put the time to good use. "I hope you saved me some." He loved the marshmallow, butter and cereal bars, hadn't had one in years.

"Of course. Mia set aside a plate of them just for you."

The thoughtfulness of his daughter never ceased to impress him. Now, if he only knew what to do about Grace.

"How was your patient?" She must have picked up on the shift in his mood, assuming it was about the post-op issue. Why would she suspect the change was about her getting too close to Mia, when he'd done nothing but encourage their interaction.

"Fine. She'd bled a bit more than expected, had loads of edema, and it freaked out the nurse. She thought she might be hemorrhaging."

"I'm glad it wasn't anything serious."

Her eyes drifted around the dim room then onto the picture of his wife. He understood that picture—right in the middle of his living room—didn't make sense. It wasn't like she could avoid looking at it.

He walked over and picked it up. "I suppose you're wondering what happened to Mia's mother."

"I won't lie. The thought has crossed my mind." She tried to smooth over her reaction by seeming nonchalant, and he was grateful. She had every right to wonder.

He sat next to her on the couch, prepared to tell her most, if not all of the story. He owed her an explanation as to why he'd flirted with her then pushed her away.

"I come from a big family, two sisters and two brothers. I'm smack in the middle. I'd always assumed I'd have lots of kids when I got married, too. But I dated a model, and the thought of having children put terror in her eyes." He raised Christie's picture to accentuate his point. "But I was crazy about her." He shrugged as his gaze roamed the living room, anything to avoid looking into Grace's eyes—as if she'd see all his darkest secrets. "I convinced her to marry me, and expected this perfect little life to play out."

Suddenly thirsty, he got up and went into the kitchen to grab himself a beer. "Can I get you something to drink?" he called out.

"I'm fine, thanks."

He popped the lid, went back to Grace and sat next to her on the couch. He offered her a drink from his can, and surprisingly she took a sip and handed it back. When he took a swig, it occurred to him that this was as close as they'd come to touching each other.

He'd missed the closeness of being with a woman. Grace looked on with inquisitive eyes, her lower legs tucked under her hip. Though normally guarded about his sad and warped tale, he knew he owed her some kind of explanation for his situation—single dad with child and a nanny, mother not in the picture.

"When I brought up the subject of kids, my wife, Christie, kept putting it off. She kept modeling."

Mitch took another drink, gave Grace a serious glance. She sat transfixed, completely ready for him to open up and tell her the rest of the story. He didn't plan to tell her everything, because the whole story was too bizarre, just enough to satisfy her curiosity.

She reached for his can and took another drink. The act of sharing a beer felt more intimate than it should, but it had been so long since he'd sat in his home with someone other than his daughter on the couch. He wanted more from Grace than she could feasibly give, especially if they were to remain colleagues. Therefore, there could never be more. End of story.

He played with the threads on her thin long-sleeved sweater. Maybe if he explained why he was so cautious about letting people close to him and Mia, she'd finally explain why she kept herself covered from neck to knees all the time. And what she'd been having Leo fix for her.

"So Christie turned twenty-nine. She swore thirty was breathing down her neck the very next day. She wanted Botox. It was ridiculous. She didn't need it. We started fighting about it." He sent Grace a cutting glance. Waited for her reaction. She played it safe and schooled her expression, obviously wanting him to continue his story. "She said everyone who modeled used it."

He glanced at the photograph, the last one he had of her before she'd started having procedures done. It still ached to think of the transition she'd made in her appearance, how he no longer recognized her.

"Then she got pregnant. I was ecstatic. Thought she'd get over that bit about striving for perfection in her looks." He gave her a rueful smile. "Boy, was I wrong. You'd have thought she'd been given a death sentence with the pregnancy. I honestly feared for our baby's life in the beginning."

Grace reached across and squeezed his knee in empathy. He patted her hand in thanks, enjoying the warmth of her skin. Though that wasn't the reason he'd opened up to Grace. He'd never use his sad tale to manipulate another woman. No. He genuinely liked and cared about Grace, and it was the strangest feeling.

"As the months went by, she couldn't cope with her body. Fell completely apart. I had to fly my two sisters down from San Francisco to L.A. to take shifts watching her, so she would eat and not harm herself or our baby. Hell, I wanted a healthy baby. She had to gain weight. That's how it works, how things are intended."

He drank more and handed the can with the last part of the beer to her. Surprisingly, she finished it with a mini-chugalug, obviously not wanting to steer his story off course or cause another delay.

"Christie insisted on a bikini cut C-section. She

wanted our baby delivered as soon as feasibly possible so she wouldn't have to get any bigger."

He gave her a doleful smile, and she returned an encouraging look. *Go on*, her eyes seemed to prod. There wasn't a hint of judgment in her sympathetic blue gaze. Her fingers were folded and touching her chin as she leaned against the couch and listened intently. She looked like an angel with dark brown bangs and such kissable lips.

"Everything changed for me once Mia was born. But not for Christie. She didn't even try to bond with our daughter. All she wanted was liposuction. We hired our first nanny then, and Christie simply handed over our child. I did as much as I could for our Mia, but I had to work, too. Sometimes long hours. I took off a couple of months in the beginning and got pretty damn good at the daddy stuff. Christie just didn't show any interest. She was self-centered and aloof. I worried how it might affect Mia emotionally later on in life."

He got that stomach cramp he always felt when he thought about Christie. On reflex, his palm drifted to his abdomen and rubbed. Grace took his hand and laced her fingers through his. He squeezed back, and the cramp let up the slightest bit.

He inhaled a ragged breath as the worst of the story was ahead. "Our marriage barely limped on, but I married for better or worse, and I'd taken those vows seriously. Most days I thought I was a fool, but…"

"You're an honorable man, Mitch. Don't ever beat yourself up for that," she said, squeezing his fingers more, making him want to pull her close and hug her for understanding so well. But he kept his distance.

"All I did was focus on Mia and work. Christie just seemed to drift out of our lives like a cold breeze. Then one day she walked out on us. Just picked up and left."

Grace covered her mouth with her hand. "Oh, my God."

"Crazy, right? I couldn't believe it." The betrayal had cut deeper than anything he'd ever experienced in life. At first, some days he hadn't thought he could breathe or live, but he'd had a daughter to look after—to be there for. He'd forced himself to carry on. Mia was his saving grace.

His eyes connected with Grace's. Could she be his other saving grace—from loneliness? Would he be crazy to let another beautiful woman close? Suddenly, everything seemed so confusing.

"Is that what brought you to the Hunter Clinic?" Her sweetly husky voice brought him back to the moment.

"In a roundabout way." He clutched the empty can and slowly but consistently strangled and smashed the aluminum. "I'd had it with all the Hollywood fakery, you know? The last thing I wanted my daughter to do was grow up surrounded by that and become superficial and self-centered like her mother. I want Mia to always know she is beautiful to me both inside and out, no matter what the blasted mirror or society says."

She gave another empathetic nod. God, he wanted to kiss her. Totally inappropriate at the moment, but there you go; he wanted those lips, the ones he'd been obsessing about since their night in the pod. *Keep on track, Cooper.*

"I'd heard about the Hunter Clinic and contacted Leo. He invited me to join. California law says you can't take a child over a state line without the consent of the other parent, let alone to another country." He gave a wry laugh. "I don't know why I was surprised when Christie didn't contest my plans. She didn't so much as lift a perfectly arched eyebrow over it. Never even came to say one last goodbye to Mia. She simply didn't give a damn."

Grace clutched her chest as if heartbroken along with him over Mia's bad luck in the mother department. He'd stopped blaming himself for choosing such a self-centered person to marry, hoped he'd change enough in the character-reading department before he'd ever invited anyone else into his life.

He'd tried to keep a distance from the emotions roiling inside him as he told the story. He hadn't opened up to anyone but his sisters about it, and it had been so long ago, and he still hadn't told the entire story tonight. Because it was too gruesome to go into. He rubbed his chest, where it still hurt like hell whenever he relived that chapter of his life.

"I packed up my daughter and made a vow that she'd never know rejection like that for the rest of her life."

Things went dead quiet. He stared at the carpet, found a small red plastic toy piece and picked it up. Set the empty and smashed beer can on the table. Anything to avoid Grace's somber stare. He felt it on the side of his face, though, and knew that eventually he'd have to look at her.

She touched his shoulder and squeezed it. "You did the right thing. Mia is an amazingly self-assured girl, and it's all thanks to you."

He glanced up seeing her total acceptance of his decision to bring his daughter to another country, leaving her mother far behind. And it meant everything to him.

But Grace was too close. Her mouth was right there....

Grace's body went hot with emotion as Mitch unraveled his story. He was a strong, admirable man for going to bat for the innocent party, his daughter. She'd never met a man like that. Mia was the most important person in Mitch's life, as every child should be to their parents.

He'd veiled his hurt by acting imperturbable, but she sensed his pain, experienced it as if it had happened to her. Her heart wrenched for both Mitch and Mia. Wanting nothing more than to comfort him, she leaned in, at eye level with his sad downward-looking eyes. His hand went to her cheek, and slowly his gaze lifted to her mouth. He traced her lower lip with the pad of his thumb, scattering warmth along her jaw. It trickled down her throat and reaching deep into her chest.

His careful yet steady gaze traveled higher, to her eyes, and seemed to ask the question, was this all right, he and her sitting on his couch, touching each other?

Only a second passed for her to make up her mind. Yes, it was. In fact, she wanted to kiss him.

Evidently, he'd beat her to the decision, as his mouth covered hers in the sweetest, sudden embrace. The physical connection sent a shock wave throughout her body.

They straightened up on the couch, leaning against the cushions, as she wrapped her hands behind his neck, pulling him nearer, pressing her lips closer, enjoying the last of his day-long scent and that evening stubble.

His warm, soft kiss almost made her forget how messed up she was. How she couldn't let anyone close. Ever again. But right now she didn't want to think about those tired old excuses, she was too wrapped up in the moment and only wanted to think about kissing Mitch.

He angled his head so their mouths fit just so, then moistened the crease of her lips with the tip of his tongue. He shifted again to feather tiny kisses around her lips and over her face, on to her earlobe for a quick nip and tug, then back to her mouth to kiss deeper, releasing a chill bomb. She relaxed, slipped into his rhythm and need, met his tongue with the tip of her own, as all resistance to his bold kiss melted away.

She sighed into the feel of his lips as he took her mouth over and over, marveling that they were kissing, and tasting the beer they'd shared, fully aware she wanted so much more with him.

But she could never have a future with a man like Mitch. With any man, especially Mitch. It was senseless to kiss him, to start anything, even though this first kiss would be tattooed in her mind for the rest of her life.

Why toy with the affections of a man with whom she couldn't be completely open? Why taunt Mitchell, who deserved a normal woman, something she could never be. He'd already met his quota of messed up, distant and damaged women with his ex-wife. That was enough for his lifetime.

She let her thoughts pull her out of the moment. Far back in her mind, she couldn't help but think he still loved his ex-wife. Why else would he keep her picture out all these years?

Mitch clutched her arms—she sensed his passion shift from exploration to need. Or maybe he'd felt her hesitation as her thoughts had wandered again and again to his ex. His kisses grew hungry, desperate. They seemed to chase after her as she mentally withdrew. His need frightened her. She could never be what he wanted. If she stayed here, he'd expect more than she could give. She couldn't bear to see the disappointment in his face if he saw her burns. It would rip her heart out.

Though she longed for the comfort and thrills his lips promised, she needed to keep it real. For her sake and for his. Kissing was an entry-level drug—it led to desire and ultimately to sex. Grace Turner didn't get naked with men any more.

She broke away from his lips, struggling to catch her breath. "No wonder they call you Lips." She hoped to lighten the mood, to smooth over the sudden end to their make-out session.

"I'd rather you didn't call me that," he said, touching her, pulling her close again.

She hadn't a clue how she'd find her way home, but she needed to get away from Mitch. She'd call a cab as soon as she could think straight.

Since the attack, it wasn't in the stars for her to live a normal life so why pretend?

"I have to get home," she said, pulling herself away from his arms.

His eyes betrayed the confusion and sexual desire he struggled to hide. "Why, Grace?"

"We can't do this, Mitch." She stood and rubbed her folded arms as if she was freezing. "It's not a good idea."

"I'm just kissing you."

Grace straightened her clothes, trying with all her power to gather her composure. "That seemed like a hell of a lot more than just kissing." She gazed at him, but couldn't withstand his smoldering stare, so she looked away. "I guess I'm not ready, then."

Her eyes found the front door and focused. She'd get to her cell phone and call that cab company. Leaving was her only hope to save face. *Get out of that door. Leave. Now.*

"I'd never push you to do anything you didn't want to." He stood and moved toward her.

"I know, but I might be the one to push myself." She inched away.

Mitch's confused expression intensified, bordering on hurt. She owed him an explanation, didn't dare give it. He'd never understand. Besides, the way he'd looked so sadly at his ex-wife's picture earlier when he'd told her the story, the way he still kept it around as if continuing to pine for her, Grace had a deep suspicion that he'd never stopped loving her.

Not even in a perfect world, under ideal circumstances—even if she were the person she'd used to be—there wouldn't be room in his life for her. His heart was still hung up on the mother of his child, and he probably didn't even know it.

She grabbed her purse off the adjacent chair and strode for the door, afraid to look back, fishing inside for her phone on the way.

She'd almost made it home free when Mitch's firm grasp on her arm swung her round.

CHAPTER SEVEN

MITCH'S MOUTH CAME crashing down on Grace's again. He kissed hard and rough this time, pushing her against the door through which she'd tried to leave.

He took her breath away, thrilling her as he fought to get her back where they'd just been, near enough to heaven to feel it. She let him have his way with her lips, not ready to end this dizzying moment. His hands skimmed every part of her arms, sides, and back as if he couldn't feel enough of her. The desperate kiss nearly broke her heart, as he seemed to pour into it every bit of emotion he'd held back during his story.

Grace understood his reckless need to have her, and it took every last bit of her self-control not to join him. To give in. To let him take her. If things had only been different…

She pushed away from his shoulders, dazed by

his ragged breath and dire need for her. Intoxicated by his palpable desire, she forced herself
to focus. This couldn't happen. They couldn't be
together, no matter how right it felt or how mes-
merizing his kisses were.

"I've got to go." Somehow she'd found her voice
as she'd ended the kiss.

He swallowed, obviously practicing self-re-
straint, and backed off. But his eyes tore into
her, stripping her naked. "Remember this." His
commanding tone dropped over her like whiskey
and honey. "Think about what we could have."

Even now, knowing she had to end it, the breath
from his voice and the nearness of him sent chills
across her shoulders and chest. Her tight breasts
ached for his attention. Every part of her cried
out for his touch.

She couldn't look another second at the messy-
haired, smoldering-eyed, sexiest man she'd ever
seen…or kissed. All she could do was turn the
knob on the door and escape.

He might have physical needs, and she understood there was definitely chemistry between
them. But as hard as it would be to open up to any

man again, to stand naked, exposed and scarred before him, she especially couldn't open herself up to heartache with a man who still loved the mother of his child.

Grace had been dreading the Cumberbatch meeting on Tuesday night. She'd managed to avoid Mitch all day thanks to a heavy surgery schedule at Kate's, but now, after hours, they'd be forced to come face-to-face because of the consultation.

It seemed everyone had left the clinic. The building was quiet and almost spooky. She wasn't even sure Mitch was on the premises.

Not wanting to be late, she'd come right to the clinic after her last surgery, and still wore scrubs. She hadn't bothered to change into street clothes and had simply thrown on her knee-length doctor's coat from her office. Tucking a thin white cotton scarf into the neckline of her top, she turned up her collar then headed down the hall to the "special" consultation room.

The clinic records verified that many a famous person had sat in this very room waiting for various minor procedures, from royalty to politician to musician to actor to reality star. The list was long, and she'd promised never to divulge their names to a soul.

With nerves skittering throughout her body, and hot memories of their kiss racing through her mind, she opened the door to find both Mitch and Davy Cumberbatch already sitting at the meeting table. Someone may as well have suddenly rung Big Ben's bell from the rush of her anxiety taking on wings and flying free at the sight of Mitch. She needed to get a grip.

Oh, and there was Davy, too.

After taking a sip of bottled water, she offered a polite smile to both men, avoiding Mitch's penetrating eyes, then used her old charm-school training to walk across the room slowly and steadily, as if she had a book balanced on her head.

Mitch stood, looking at her as if he hadn't seen her since forever, ravenously eating her up with his eyes. His gaze ran hot, oozing with longing, then pulled back to a fully professional expression.

She'd been transported back to last night, was

right there with him on the desire level, seeing him for the first time since their kisses. The mere thought sparked a pool of heat, its warm rivulets coursing throughout her body. Her cheeks grew hot. She needed another drink of water and took it before sitting down.

Finally, she looked at Davy, who hadn't bothered to stand, just sat there like a prince without manners. Gaunt, his sallow skin showing the evidence of hard living and self-indulgence, it seemed hard to imagine the legions of loyal fans he'd made over the past three decades. The image she'd been working with on her computer must have been several years back, in a healthier time. That could prove to be a problem, and further reason for her to refuse him his wish.

"Mr. Cumberbatch, I'm a big fan, it's a pleasure to meet you." She'd take one for the clinic and lie through her teeth, mark it off as being a team player.

Life came back to his battered face. He smiled. "Hey, Doc." He glanced at Mitchell. "You didn't tell me about the hot doc."

Grace could tell Mitch had reverted to diplo-

198 200 HARLEY STREET: AMERICAN SURGEON IN LONDON

matic skills for the sake of the Hunter Clinic, as she had. He forced a smile, though she'd glimpsed a flash of anger in his charm. "We don't like to divulge all our secrets. You can relate to that, right, Davy?" Mitch winked.

The sarcasm and condescension skidded right over Davy's over-dyed elfin-styled punk hairdo, which seemed a tad ridiculous on a fortysomething male in the first place. She couldn't quite bring herself to call him a man, since his reputation remained more in the petulant and spoiled-boy realm. The sad thing was, if she'd been bold enough to tell him what she really thought, he'd just laugh and take it to the bank. Why should he care what anyone thought of him, when he was rolling in dough from his well-documented antics?

Finally, introductions were over and Grace took a calming breath, fighting the need to use disinfectant on her hands. "Let's get right down to business, okay?"

Davy nodded. Mitch sat straight and stiff, palms opened and flat against the table, wearing a well-rehearsed poker face.

Grace flipped open her laptop and went directly to the graphic program and the file she'd created on Davy Cumberbatch.

She showed him his natural face, before the recent barroom brawl, then superimposed the mock-up of his surgical cosmetic requests. After a few magic keystrokes his face morphed into an odd combination of the artist formerly known as Cumberbatch and the king of rock and roll, Elvis.

She used her big-guns software to create a 3D effect then rotated the virtual head three-sixty degrees so he could see himself from all angles. It wasn't a pretty sight, far from a match made in cyberland. On the contrary, the image on the computer screen looked near grotesque. More like a cartoon character. Grace used this graphic to drive home her point.

"As you can see, what you think you want isn't in your best interest." Without waiting for the stunned expression to fade from his face, she flipped to another screen and a far more agreeable rendition of Davy the rocker. At least, she thought so. "In this version, I've toned down the heavy Elvis influence and allowed the natural characteristics of your face to remain, giving a hint of the king but not superimposing your face with his. We can also remove some of the adipose tissue from above and beneath your eyes to give you a more youthful appearance."

"Adi-what?"

"Fat. See here and here?"

She pointed out his puffy lids and bags, waited for him to take a look.

"I've also given you some nips here and tucks there…" she gestured toward his real-life jaw and cheeks then focused back on the computer screen "…slenderized your nose, shortened and shaped the tip in a more classical way, and made the cheek implants smaller than your original request. But they work very nicely, don't you think?"

She swallowed and looked his way. Davy narrowed his eyes and studied the second computer image, not saying a word—though he didn't look happy. He glanced at Mitchell, as if he'd step in and make things right, put the "hot doc" in her place.

Davy turned back toward Grace. "It doesn't

look a bit like Elvis, does it?" He hit her with a deadly stare, and she refused to look away. She'd be damned if she'd let him bully her.

Grace braced herself for a fight. And she'd surely lose if Mitch took Davy's side and they ganged up on her. Did Mitch really believe in giving the patient whatever they wanted no matter how bizarre the outcome?

She took a breath and held it, using all of her control and concentration not to blink.

"I agree with Miss Turner, Davy." Mitch broke the standoff, utilizing his natural affable charm. She breathed again and shifted her eyes to his, wanting to thank him. "The second image is far more complimentary to you." He tore his glance away from Grace and homed in on Davy. "And though you won't look like Elvis, let's be honest—could anyone? The point I believe Miss Turner is making is do you want to be the new and improved Davy Cumberbatch or a caricature of someone else for the rest of your life? It's your call."

Grace wanted to hug Mitch on the spot. Oh, wait, that wouldn't be a good idea after last night.

She flashed him a quick smile, but yanked it back immediately, not wanting to come off smug in front of the rocker. That would be like coming down to his level and there was no way she could compete with Davy Cumberbatch when it came to being pompous.

Davy slumped down in the luxurious white leather club chair, giving the impression of a defeated teenager. Sullen, looking as if he'd just swallowed castor oil. "You made me go through rehab for this? I told you I wanted Elvis, and I always get what I want." He spoke through clenched teeth, his ring-covered fingers tightly balled into fists on the table.

Grace instinctively moved back in her chair, bracing herself, as if another brawl might break out.

"Very well," Mitchell said. "I'll refer you to another top-notch plastic surgeon, one more willing to give you exactly what you want." Mitchell stood, and reached out his hand for a shake. "Unfortunately, it won't be here at the Hunter Clinic."

Davy took his time getting up, his lanky legs seeming a bit wobbly. He never completed the handshake, just blew off Mitch's proffered hand. Once he'd made it to his full height, several inches shorter than Mitch, he glanced upward with something short of hatred coloring his dark, tiny, deep-set eyes.

Then he glanced her way. The biting stare made Grace swallow hard, tightening her core. She would not let him get the best of her. Angry that she'd given him the power to make her feel uncomfortable, she got up and stepped close to him, then looked into those stabbing eyes. "I hope you'll reconsider." She tried her best to sound professionally earnest, hoping to overcome both his ire and the anger burning inside her. Why should she care? "I'll forward my graphics to your personal email. Maybe you'd like to have another look at them and think about how you'd like to look from now on."

He brushed her off, the mark of a man who had little regard for women outside of groupies, and then only because he wanted sex with them, and engaged Mitch's attention. "I'll think about it. Get back to you."

One moment a hot doc, the next she didn't exist.

The Hunter Clinic was known for profession-alism, and though Grace wanted to knee the guy in his groin, she stood her ground and let Mitch take over.

"Oh, first I guess we'd better put an eye patch on you," he said. "Get our story straight about you having a small tear in the retina and needing our help in the ophthalmology room." He patted his pockets then glanced at Grace. "Do you have the prepared statement from Lexi?"

Mitch strode to the stainless-steel supply cart in the middle of the otherwise posh consultation area, found an eye patch then used tape to hold it in place on Davy's face.

While he did that, she made a quick scan through her emails. There it was, the PR state-ment. "Give me a moment and I'll print it out." With the click of a finger from her laptop, the copier in the corner of the room came to life and spit out one page, a short and sweet statement. She retrieved it and brought it to Mitch as he put the finishing touches on Davy's eye patch.

"There, you look like a regular pirate. Now, repeat after me. I had a small tear in my retina and needed laser surgery to repair it."

Davy refused—what else was new?—but nodded. "Got it."

Mitch took the proffered statement and escorted Davy out to where Grace assumed Davy's people waited, but not before passing her a look loaded with meaning.

She could barely take it.

Their kiss came clearly to mind, and her body reacted as if it was actually in his embrace again, feeling his lips pressed to hers. She forced herself to stop the silliness. It simply could never be between them. The only kind of partners they'd ever be was at work in the operating room.

But even seeing him only as a colleague, she still could have grabbed and kissed Mitch when he'd come to her aid just now. He'd given her opinion some thought and apparently agreed with her. The man respected her opinion. Surely there was a point where any good surgeon drew the line.

Her heart lurched as she thought of Mitch

standing up for her. She smiled at his quirky sense of humor—Davy as a pirate, hardly!

Mitch Cooper was appealing on far, far too many levels.

The room seemed suddenly buzzing with thoughts and questions and feelings with which she wasn't ready to deal. The lights were too bright, and the room felt hot and stuffy with left-over Cumberbatch soiling the air. She had to get out.

With Mitch and Davy gone, she took the opportunity to close her laptop, grab her purse and slip out the side door, heading straight for home.

Yes, she was a coward for not sticking around to tell Mitch in person how much she appreciated him backing her up. But the thought of what might happen after last night's passion and the possibility of letting Mitch get closer again tonight scared her. What if she opened up to him, had sex with him, and he pretended her scars didn't bother him? When she knew with all her heart they would. How could they not?

His lies and pity would rip her wide open.

* * *

The paparazzi at the back of the building were out of control. Cameras flashed and questions flew their way the instant the bodyguard opened the alley exit to the clinic. The chauffeur made a beeline for the limo and the bodyguard protected Davy from as many clean shots at picture-taking as possible.

"Why'd you come here tonight, Davy?"

When there was no response they turned to Mitchell.

"Tell us why Davy was here, Doctor."

Mitch glanced at Davy, being rushed to his car, not saying a word. He decided to run with the preplanned script from Lexi. "Mr. Cumberbatch suffered an eye injury and needed some laser surgery to mend a small tear in his retina." There was more to read, about how the Hunter Clinic hoped they'd fixed his injury to his satisfaction, blah, blah, blah, but before they could ask another question, Mitch turned for the door. At that exact moment another flurry of flashing lights indicated the limo was leaving the premises.

Mitch looked back and watched Davy Cumberbatch drive off in his white limousine, with one over-enthusiastic gossip rag photographer hanging from the bumper.

"Get the hell off the car, you idiot." The bodyguard had stood up in the middle of the sky light and flipped the finger at the reporters. More cameras flashed. No doubt there'd be plenty of pictures for the gossip rags tomorrow. The limo sped up and left the alley.

Mitch closed the heavy door tight, bolted and locked it.

He still seethed with the way Davy had brushed off Grace's hard work. She had state-of-the-art computer programs, computer software that he certainly wouldn't be able to operate without weeks of tutorials. She must have spent hours and hours putting the presentation together. Yes, she'd been blunt with Davy, but kind; the guy had acted like a spoiled brat. He'd like to throttle the old rocker, but had simply stood and waved goodbye like a moron in the night.

Mitch made his way back inside, eager to see Grace again, wanting nothing more than to apologize for his entire gender. What an ass that guy was. When their eyes had first met before the meeting had begun he'd almost come out of his seat with desire. It had been years and years since he'd felt that way about a woman…not since his ex-wife.

He swallowed back the longing for Grace, especially after the way she'd made her quick getaway last night. She'd literally run off into the night, phone to ear, calling a cab and walking toward the corner crossing. He'd wanted to run after her, but hadn't wanted to leave Mia alone in the house. He'd called out to her, begged her to come back, but she'd refused.

"I'm sorry," she'd said. "I need to go."

From inside his house he'd watched for over ten minutes as she'd paced beneath a streetlamp, until finally the cab had arrived, and he'd been able to breathe properly again.

Their kisses had been filled with passion, reaching so deep inside him he'd almost felt they'd joined together. Now all he could think about was finishing the act they'd played out with kisses, only this time using the rest of their bodies.

He'd wanted her with every cell crying out for

her mercy, and was almost positive she'd wanted him, too. But for some reason she'd lost it, pulled back. Damn, after the sad story he'd told her, could he blame her?

Unless she was afraid of being close to a man.

Maybe he could change her mind.

He rushed down the last few steps of the hallway. He grabbed the handle and opened the door...only to find the room empty.

Disappointment cut through him, triggering anger. Twice now she'd run off to avoid him. If he hadn't kissed her, felt how deeply she'd responded to him, he might think she wanted nothing to do with him. But he'd been there with her, kissing like the world might end tomorrow. Her heated response had stirred up the hunger he'd suppressed for years, making him lust after her until his bed sheets were damp and twisted from restless sleep.

He wouldn't take no for an answer without a really good reason, and she couldn't keep avoiding him for ever. When she finally stopped running from him, he'd be there, waiting to take her to his bed.

He flipped off the lights, locked up the room and left the Hunter Clinic as fast as humanly possible. He planned to go directly to Grace's apartment to confront her, force her to see how right they were for each other, see where it led.

On the way to his car his cell phone rang. It was Roberta. Mia refused to go to bed until Daddy read her a story and tucked her in.

Grace dried her hair, the noise of the dryer helping to drown out her thoughts. She'd imagined Mitch during the entire shower, wondered what it would be like to be naked with him, to be touched by him. All over.

This had to stop. She could no more expose herself to Mitch than he could pretend her scars didn't exist. She forced a look in the mirror at her chest and arms with webs of white and pink marbling scars where the acid had eaten away her skin. She'd lost count of the number of skin grafts she'd had to endure those first few years. The pain, both external and internal.

What man would want to make love to breasts like hers? How would the roughened skin on her arms feel to Mitch's touch? Could he want her sexually after seeing everything?

She looked away, put on her robe and distracted herself by continuing to blow-dry her hair.

It never failed. Why did the phone ring whenever she used the dryer? Like right now. She wasn't going to fall for it because it would only be another false alarm. It always was.

On she blew and brushed her hair, forcing the waves into submission.

When she was done, she put special aloe-and-vitamin-E-extract lotion across her neck, chest and arms, especially around the recently touched-up section at the base of her neck and collarbone. Then she used her favorite vanilla-and-lavender cream on her legs. Feeling fresh after a long day at the hospital, she walked to the kitchen to make some herbal tea. She put the kettle on to boil and put a pyramid-shaped tea bag into her favorite yellow-flowered cup, then started shuffling around in the cupboard for something to nibble on.

The intercom sounded. She jumped.

A burst of nerves warned she couldn't get away

from Mitch that easily. He was probably upset about how she'd pressed Davy Cumberbatch to be realistic with his cosmetic surgery. He'd probably only backed her up to help save face for the clinic, but had come here to have words about her performance at the clinic.

Or he was here about last night—and the passion they'd shared. The thought released pent-up tingles across the very skin she'd just loaded with cream.

After stomping out the quick desire to take the coward's way out by not answering, she padded across the carpet. She was a fully grown woman who needed to confront her issues head on. The list of reasons she would never become intimate with Mitch started with the fact he was still in love with his ex-wife, included her scars, and ended with the very major point that they worked together.

"Who is it?" She prayed she was wrong, and it wasn't Mitch but someone else.

"It's Mitch."

So much for prayers. She wasn't dressed. "You should have called first."

"I did. You didn't answer."

The damn hairdryer. "Can you give me a minute? I'm just out of the bath."

"Let me in."

He sounded nothing like the man she'd grown to know and adore. All playfulness was gone from his voice. He sounded angry. She *had* botched things up with Cumberbatch.

"Please," he finally added.

Without saying a word, she pressed the door release, heard it buzz and him quickly enter her building. She flipped up the collar and lapels on her thick white robe, tied the sash around her waist, rushed to the bathroom and grabbed a towel, throwing it over her shoulders, clutching it tightly to her throat.

She didn't need to be dressed to tell Mitch to forget they'd ever kissed. Or stare him in the eye and tell him she'd treat her patients the way she saw fit, no matter how famous they were. Whichever scenario played out, she was ready. She double-knotted the sash on her robe and for security's sake went immediately back to clutching the towel.

His rapid knock at the door forced her out of the bathroom. She needed to get it together before she faced him. Two feet from the door she stopped and took a deep inhale, a cleansing breath. She held it for a beat and felt her pulse slow the slightest bit. *Stay calm. Act like nothing has happened. Just another day on the job.*

She swung open the door. "Cooper! What brings you here?"

He looked her over, his lips pursed, eyes consuming her. She needed another cleansing breath, quickly!

He didn't bother to answer her, just walked into her apartment like he lived there. Maybe he'd been taking lessons from Cumberbatch.

"Well?" she said.

"Well, what?"

"I asked what brings you here?"

"I would have been here earlier if I hadn't gotten a call from Roberta."

"The nanny? Is something wrong with Mia?" Her sudden concern reminded her how much she'd come to care for the child.

"Just a minor catastrophe." For the first time

since she'd opened the door he showed a glimpse of his usual self. "Couldn't find her favorite book for bedtime."

"*The Tale of Misty Do-Right in the Battle of the Wrongs?*"

He nodded. "You remember?"

"How could I forget such great literature?"

He smiled, studied her more. "You look beautiful tonight."

"You're out of your mind. I've just gotten out of the bath and my hair is a fright."

He grabbed the wrist she'd waved around to brush off his statement. "My eyesight is perfect." The hunger in his eyes almost made her believe him.

She took back her hand. "Stop it, please."

He hesitated then shifted back to serious mode. "Look, we need to talk."

"About?" She couldn't manage to hold her robe tight enough but didn't want him to notice her white knuckles, so she lightened her grip.

"Us."

The kettle had boiled and rather than respond

to him she dashed to the kitchen, pretending she hadn't heard what he'd said. Us? Oh, no.

"Would you like some tea?" she called over her shoulder, but hadn't needed to raise her voice after all because he was right there, standing behind her.

"No."

She begged her mind to stay focused and her hands to function as she poured steaming hot water into her cup. "I really need to thank you for sticking up for me with that vile Cumberbatch earlier."

Silence.

"Did I blow it for the clinic?" She peeked over her shoulder, saw a man who wasn't interested in office chitchat, a man who looked as serious as hell.

"Why did you push me away last night? Why did you leave?"

She used the granite counter for balance before slowly turning round. Nothing like getting right to the point. *Tell him the truth.* "Because it doesn't make sense to get involved with a man who's still in love with his ex-wife."

Okay, so that was half of the truth.

Disbelief twisted his brows and wrinkled his nose. "How could you possibly think I still love my ex-wife after what I've told you?"

"Have you dated since moving to England?"

A sheepish look passed over his exquisitely handsome features. "Yes. I made the mistake of getting involved with one of the nurses at the Hunter Clinic a few months after I arrived. Things didn't work out. She eventually changed jobs."

"And that was how long ago?"

"Look, I've dated a few women since then, nothing serious, but nevertheless. The thing is, I don't want to confuse Mia."

She swallowed the ball of emotion forming in her throat. "You still keep your ex-wife's picture out, and I saw how you looked at her. I was sure I saw love in your eyes."

"For a person who doesn't exist anymore! She didn't want our daughter, remember? How can I love a monster like that?"

"She's not a monster, Mitch, she's a broken person. We're all damaged in some ways." She glanced at the angry scar peeking out from the sleeve of her robe and quickly covered it.

He shook his head and gazed at her with a pained expression. "You don't know the whole story. I thought I'd told you enough to make you understand. Obviously, I didn't go far enough."

This was her chance to get to the heart of the issue. If his ex-wife was so evil, she had to know. "Then why do you keep her picture out?"

"For Mia's sake. A child needs to know who her parents are. Christie is her mother."

She took a moment to engage his eyes. All she wanted to do was level with him, he deserved her honesty. "Okay, but maybe you're still hoping she'll come back, be the mother Mia needs, the wife you still pine for."

Hadn't he alluded to that the very first night they'd met at the Eye, after they'd gone to the bar then he'd seen her off in the taxi? *If it was a different time in my life. If circumstances were different. The thing is...it wouldn't be fair.*

It wouldn't be fair because he still loved his ex-wife.

"God, you are so wrong. You don't know what

you're talking about." He sounded frustrated, and a little angry. "Christie isn't the woman in that picture anymore. She's a totally different person. Some freakish creation…" he used his hands as if juggling balls searching for the right description "…from a surgeon's scalpel."

Grace shook her head, not wanting to understand. Had someone cut up Christie's face?

"Just before she got pregnant, she started having little cosmetic procedures. Laser treatments on tiny old chicken-pox scars, Botox injections, skin bleaching—you name it, she wanted to try it."

Mitch walked to the kitchen table, pulled out a chair and sat, resting on his elbows. Grace leaned her back against the counter and sipped her tea, prepared for a long story and eager to hear every last bit of it.

"I told her she was perfect just the way she was, but she didn't see it. Every fine line was blown out of proportion to being her death sentence as a model. She wanted me to give her a nose job. When I refused, she wanted me to refer her to the best plastic surgeons, and when I fought her about having rhinoplasty, she snuck off to my partner."

Grace could imagine how infuriating it would be to deal with an already beautiful woman who wanted nothing more than to be even more beautiful. Especially if he was married to her.

Mitch stared at the tiled floor, as if reliving a horrible secret. He alternated rubbing his knuckles with his palms, first one hand than the other. She didn't know how he could possibly talk with his jaw muscles bunched so tightly.

"She kept sneaking off to Rick." He looked up, realizing she might need an explanation. "My business partner and best friend, by the way." He tossed her another quick glance loaded with hurt and defeat.

"Christie was never satisfied with how she looked after that first operation. I suspect she already knew she'd blown it and ruined what she'd been given naturally, but wouldn't stop. Could never go back. But, oh, how she tried."

Grace understood exactly what he spoke of— she'd seen it in far too many cosmetic surgery patients, which was exactly why she'd specialized in reconstructive surgery instead.

Mitch turned sideways in the chair, leaned forward, elbows on his thighs, hands locked and head down. "Her vanity astounded me at times, but that's what I got for only dating models when I was a bachelor. I was just as vain about my women as she was about her looks. Until Mia came along."

He glanced up, a look of shame and regret coloring his eyes.

"At least you saw it, Mitch, saw the superficiality of it all. You became a parent, rose to the occasion. But last night you said Christie wasn't able to."

"God, no. Christie kept having more surgery, especially after Mia. I already told you that part but, damn, I just kept hoping she'd come to her senses before it was too late. And, honestly, it already was too late. She'd ruined her face, striving for perfection. Had at least three nose jobs." He scrubbed fingers through his hair. "I lost count."

He hung his head. Things went silent for a few moments. Grace didn't dare utter a sound, so as not to stop him. He needed to get this nightmare off his chest, and if all she could be for him was a friend and a sounding board, she'd gladly be that.

She studied Mitch, a gorgeous man on the outside, one who'd once been just as superficial as his wife, but who'd grown up when he'd become a father. She had to respect a man who learned the importance of being a parent, and the true priorities in life. They went much deeper than the skin. Oh, God, if only she could believe that about herself.

"After that, Christie was a stranger to me." He broke into her thoughts. "And she looked like a plastic doll instead of a woman. I had to let her do her thing or I'd have lost the mother of my child and my wife altogether. I thought I'd taken the high road, was doing her a huge favor by not throwing her out." He cleared his throat, stared at his shoes. "But the joke was on me. She left. Me. For Rick. The guy who kept whittling away at what was left of her natural beauty. My so-called best friend."

Grace stifled the gasp in her throat. Poor Mitch. He'd done the right thing and been double-crossed. This amazing surgeon before her was as broken as she was. She wanted to rush to his side and hold him, but that might send a message that she wasn't prepared to follow through on. Moisture formed in her eyes and she bit her lower lip instead of physically offering him comfort.

"Obviously I couldn't work with Richard as my partner any more. I sold him the business and left Hollywood." He looked up and noticed her tears. She saw how they took him aback, his thick lashes dipping and lifting in quick succession. He took a breath and let it out in a long and tired huff.

"If I have any feelings left for Christie, they are for who she used to be, that person in the picture, long before I realized how self-centered and selfish she truly was. That woman is long gone, probably never really was, and I can assure you I'm over her." He waited for Grace to look at him again. His eyes had softened, and the tension etched in his forehead had disappeared, as if telling his story had freed him. "Believe me, Grace, I am completely and truly over her."

"I believe you." She put her cup on the counter and took a couple steps toward him, taking his hand and squeezing it. The warmth from their laced-together fingers traveled up her arms.

"I need you to believe something else, too." He rose to be closer to eye level with her.

She tilted her head upward, delving into his steady gaze. How much more could there be to his heartrending story?

He lightened the grip and gently held her hands, then stared into her eyes until she thought she might faint from the powerful jolt it sent through her. She'd never noticed how his green eyes were outlined in a ring of dark hazel, and how his thick, short lashes clumped together in an almost sawtooth fashion. She could gaze into his eyes for hours and hours and never grow bored.

"Since I've met you…" He pulled her close and wrapped his arms tightly around her. She welcomed the warmth and strength of his chest. "I've come back to life." The words vibrated in his chest as he spoke with his jaw beside her head. "I trust my instinct again, and know that you are good and true, and beautiful inside and out." He kissed the top of her head then took her by the arms and moved her away enough so he could look into her eyes again. A tender smile gently curved his mouth.

"You've restored my faith in women."

Now he'd gone too far. "Oh, go on." She couldn't help herself, a tiny bubble of joy and disbelief slipped from between her lips. He'd practically claimed she'd saved mankind.

"I mean it, Gracie." He tilted her head so she could see the sincerity in his eyes, those beautiful dark-as-the-forest eyes. She stilled, taking in every word.

"Because of you I believe in love again."

CHAPTER EIGHT

MITCH CUPPED GRACE'S face and planted a kiss on her. She knew she should fight it, but though it had only been twenty-four hours since the last time, she'd already missed the feel and pressure of his lips. She'd missed the smooth glide of the inside of his mouth and the velvety feel of his tongue as he searched out hers. His flavor was passion and the faintest bit of wintergreen mixed with the herbal hibiscus she'd just sipped.

He tasted so good. She could kiss him for hours.

He'd bared his soul to her. Accused her of changing the world for him, as if she were a superhero or a goddess. Only the intimacy of sex would bring them closer, but she couldn't let herself think about that, getting naked, baring it all in front of him; she didn't want to ruin the moment.

The kiss took on a life of its own. Needful.

Intense. Frantic. The towel dropped from her shoulders, and she didn't care. His mouth and strong jaw took control. She answered his delving tongue with explorations of her own, and he obviously liked her nipping and tugging on his lips.

His hands grazed her hips and squeezed. A tiny moan escaped her throat, filling the otherwise quiet room with another heady sound besides their fierce kisses. His breathing went ragged; she nearly panted as her body came to life. Every nerve ending lit up, pulsing across her skin, leaving trails of tiny goose bumps. Warm jets of need invaded her secret lair. The weight of her robe became heavy and intrusive. If only she could take it off.

"I need you," Mitch said, pulling her hips close to his. His thickening length pressed against her, nothing but his clothes separating them. She parted her robe to bring him closer.

He was as emotionally damaged as she as. She knew the whole twisted tale. They were two wounded people with the chance to share a blissful timeout from the rest of their lives. Maybe together they could forget.

Could she trust him?

Why did she have to carry her brokenness on her skin? She wanted to scream out for the thousandth time at the sick bastard who'd meant to hurt her sister.

"Grace." Mitchell must have sensed her change. The inner turmoil threatened to ruin things again and again. No man could put up with it for long. He'd quit kissing her, loosening his hold, looking puzzled. "Have I done something?"

"No. This is good." All she wanted to do was go back to their kissing, back to forgetting everything else, if her mind would only cooperate, but he wouldn't let her.

"What's happened? I told you I wanted you and you tensed up. I don't want to push myself on you, but you've got to know how much I want—"

"Nothing's happened. Please, Mitch, kiss me." She stepped back into his arms, but he wouldn't hold her. Oh, no, now she'd blown everything.

His gaze penetrated her eyes, as if searching for the truth. His stare slowly traveled down to her neck. He lifted the hair from her shoulder, folded down the collar of her robe where she knew a scar peeked above, and moved in for a kiss. She tensed again.

He stopped. "Is this what you've been seeing Leo about?"

Surprised, she nodded.

But she couldn't bear it. Soon he'd notice the extent of her scarred flesh. She had to think fast. She wanted nothing more than to make love with Mitch, for once to leave her mind out of it, let her body take control. But she couldn't let him see her for the first time like this, not under the glaring kitchen light.

Maybe in the dark…

She stepped back, shook her head, so her hair covered her neck again, then managed a smile. "Why don't we go into the bedroom?" Without waiting for an answer, she took his hand and led him across the kitchen, down the short hall to her room. She opened the door, smiled over her shoulder at the man she planned to lure into the dark. At least there, in the dark, she wouldn't be able to see his reaction when he realized how scarred she was.

She wanted this time with Mitch more than she

could ever remember. Once outside her room, seeing the heat still in his eyes, she breathed a sigh of relief, knowing it wasn't too late.

Grace drew Mitch over the threshold, using only her fingertips. Once he was inside she closed the door and turned off the lights. But before she could remove her hand from the switch plate, his covered hers. Her fingers went still as he turned the lights back on.

Caught and cornered, she looked pleadingly at him.

"Talk to me," he said.

"What *don't* you want me to see?" *A surgical scar?* Mitch guessed. Was that what Leo had been fixing? "How shallow do you think I am?" He glanced toward her neck, remembering how she always kept it covered. Her motionless stare registered dread. He moved her thick, silky hair away again, and tried to pull the white spa robe from her shoulder. "Do you think a little scar can scare me off?"

Wild hands stopped him. He froze. She'd invited him into her bedroom, yet now he'd stepped over the line? He shook his head, confused but desperately wanting to understand.

"You don't know what you're saying," she said.

With tears brimming, she looked defeated and distraught, not anything close to the way a woman seducing a man would. The sight of her, nearly begging him to stop asking questions, made him feel queasy. What had he done but follow her into her bedroom and turn on the lights? Hadn't she invited him inside?

He pulled back his hands, holding up his palms, making a physical promise not to touch her right now. "Tell me," he whispered. "Tell me what I don't know."

She swallowed and looked down. All he wanted to do was hold her, tell her everything would be all right, but he wouldn't dare touch her again until he knew she wanted him to. Her obvious despair tore at his emotions.

She worried her mouth, as if fighting to hold in the explanation he demanded. Yet he had no intention of leaving without one.

Her eyelids closed halfway. She stared into nothingness. "I was burned by acid."

The words trickled out without a hint of animation.

Yet she may as well have hit him with a sledgehammer. Her matter-of-fact statement nearly threw him off balance. He leaned against the wall for support. Anger and pain twined and exploded in his gut. Something told him not to show the feelings roiling through him, that she needed him to be restrained. He fought his instinct to grab and hold her with all his might, to honor hers.

"Go on." His voice was measured.

"Twelve years ago my sister started college, and immediately fell in love with the wrong guy." She stood perfectly still, reciting her history. "Hope realized it too late, after the guy became obsessed with her. He questioned everything she did, was jealous of anyone else she spent time with, and essentially became a paranoid freak. She kept it to herself, until one night when we had an online video call and I could see how stressed out she was. I begged her to do something about it."

She stared toward the distant corner, numbness in her eyes, as though she was exhausted from reciting the events that had happened years before.

"I was already home for summer break and knew Hope planned to break up with Tyler just before she came home from university. She thought everything had gone well, until one day he showed up at our house, demanding to see her. To talk to her." Grace lifted her arms, the first body movement since she'd started opening up, and used air quotes around "talk to her," said it in a clipped, angry manner—the first sign of emotion since she'd begun.

"I didn't trust him and refused to leave the room. Hope told me to go, but as I suspected she only said it to appease Tyler, because I could see it, the terror in her eyes. I snuck around the back of the house and watched through the French doors."

Grace crossed the room and sat on the edge of her bed, looking wrung out. The ache in his chest got stronger, seeing the normally full-of-life woman he'd been so fascinated with these past few weeks look deflated and defeated. He forced himself not to run to her side, to keep the distance for her sake. Nothing must stop her from telling the whole story. He deserved to hear it and she obviously needed to get it off her chest.

She picked at her robe with one hand, clutching the collar with the other. "I couldn't hear them, but from my vantage point I could see the pleading, fear and anger on my sister's face. She was sticking to her guns and refusing to get back together with him, just like she told me she already had at school. My fingers were ready to hit Emergency on my cell phone."

She paused.

Mitch wondered if her mind tried to rewind and change the outcome, even as she told the story. He wished he had the power to do it for her.

"Tyler must have realized he couldn't bully her into getting what he wanted anymore. Then I saw him reach into his back pocket for a brown glass bottle." She stopped briefly, closed her eyes as if shutting out horrible thoughts, the burden of knowing what would happen next.

"I didn't know what it was, but he was a science major and instinct told me to bolt into that room and knock it out of his hand before he could do anything to harm Hope. I tried to push him away as he uncapped and splashed the acid. Hope jumped back. He shifted and aimed the bottle toward me." She clenched her eyes tightly closed, wringing moisture from the sides. "He got me instead."

Fury rose up in Mitch's gut. What monster could do such a thing? For the first time in his life he suspected he was capable of killing someone.

Tears streaked down her cheek. She'd done the noble thing of protecting her sister from a crazy person and had paid the price with her own flesh. Tiny pins pricked behind Mitch's eyes, moisture gathered and brimmed on his lids. He ached to hold Grace and tell her how beautiful she was, even as he imagined smashing in the face of the maniac who'd done this to her. His fists opened and closed. *Please tell me the sick bastard's in jail.*

Sensing she wasn't through, he used every fiber of restraint and held firm where he was, leaning against the wall, keeping quiet, knuckles nearly cramping.

"I missed a semester of med school during the

trial, but was determined to make up for it once I'd healed. Since then I've gone through countless skin grafts and extensive plastic surgery. But nothing will ever take away all of these scars."

"It doesn't matter," he said quietly.

"Yes, it does." She pleaded with him with her stare. "I was in love and engaged to be married back then. Ben was the greatest guy in the world. At least, that's what I thought. He'd stayed by my side throughout the hospital stay, coming every day, bundling up in gowns and gloves just so he could hold my hand when I was in isolation."

Her jaw tightened and her chin quivered. "But I was always bandaged up, and when we were finally together—" emotion bubbled from her throat, she fought it back "—he was horrified. Didn't want to touch me. Couldn't. I mean, why would he? I looked like uncooked meat back then." She hung and shook her head. "How could I blame him?" She bit her lower lip and swallowed. "I haven't been intimate with anyone since. Can't take the risk. Besides, who would want me?" She squeezed her eyes closed again. "I never want to see that look again."

Finally she glanced at Mitch, offering him a doleful smile. "I'm afraid you're still looking for perfection, and the sight of me will ruin things between us."

She'd finally said it: she was afraid to show herself to him. She was willing to make love to him in the dark, because she didn't want to see his reaction. Oh, God, how could he make her know he didn't give a damn about the status of her skin? It was her, her heart and soul, that he wanted.

"I'm a surgeon, Grace. I've seen it all. Nothing could shock me, surely you understand that?"

"Did you hear anything I just said?" A puff of air pushed through her lips. Her face contorted. She peeked out from between tightly clenched eyelids. "He couldn't look at me. My scars turned him completely off."

"I'm not him. You've got to trust me, my love. Whatever that jerk's name was, he didn't deserve you. All I see is beauty when I look at you. You've got to believe that nothing can stop me from loving you."

"I can't live through another rejection like that ever again."

He shook his head, his body covered from head to toes with chills. Overcome, emotion flowed so powerfully he couldn't speak. Only one thing occurred to him. He had to show her how he felt about her, how her inner beauty was a hundred times stronger than her scars. She was the most beautiful, authentic person he'd ever known and nothing, nothing—especially her scars—could ever change that opinion.

Mitch came to her. He looked at her as if she were the most beautiful woman in the universe. There wasn't a hint of pity in those sea-green eyes, shiny with moisture and empathy. It seemed all wrong, his sexy intent. How could he still find her attractive? But his determined expression almost made her believe him.

Trust flickered in her chest. "Don't pity me. Please, don't."

He dropped onto one knee as she sat on the edge of her bed, and took her hand, looking sincerely into her eyes. "How can I pity you when I love you? All I see when I look at you is the most beautiful human being I've ever met."

She went still. He knew everything and he still wanted her.

Without another word he turned her hand over and kissed her palm, then her wrist, sending warm ribbons up her arm. He eased up the long sleeve of her robe, and she didn't fight him. Wouldn't. She had nothing else to hide. He knew her story, what he was getting into, what he'd find—scars, scars, and more scars.

It didn't matter anymore.

He feathered kisses up the inside of her arm, stopping at the delicate spot in the bend of her elbow, taking his time, giving her undivided attention there. Contrary to what she'd believed about her scars all these years, she wasn't numb but felt every touch of his lips as he burned his way north.

Prickles tiptoed on nerve endings, up her body, erupting into tingles on the back of her neck and across her shoulders. Her breasts tightened. The natural-as-breathing response made her dare to believe again. She smiled just as Mitch's eyes drifted upward. Their gazes held and melded, and, as sure as she'd ever been about anything, she knew he still wanted her. From his smoldering stare, the message was loud and clear that he couldn't live one more second without making love to her.

She wiped the stale tears from her eyes and basked in these new feelings, her anxiety and doubt seeping out, the leftover resistance vaporizing one touch at a time. He released what was left of her clutch on the spa robe and slid it off, first one shoulder then the other, kissing the base of her neck, the top of her arm, the webbed white scars on her breastbone. And, yes, alive again, she felt all of it.

Grace held her breath, waiting for him to change his mind.

Instead, he cupped her jaw with one hand, fingered a clump of her hair with the other, and stared her down as if she belonged to him. "You're beautiful." His mouth bussed hers. "So beautiful."

He caressed her breast, gently lifting, admiring—kissing her there. And there. Making her almost believe she *was* beautiful.

She dug her fingers into his thick dark hair, as she'd longed to so many times before, and pulled his head to her chest. Feeling his breath against her skin, she savored the moment. He found her nipple, flicked with his tongue then kissed it, tugging lightly, releasing another wave of chills she wasn't prepared for.

She liked feeling unprepared, her head swimming with sensation.

She kissed his head, inhaling the rich sent of his hair, getting lost in the feel of his hands as they explored her ribs, her waist. Her belly. He didn't act like a man horrified by her scars—or a man who pitied her. The lights were on. He could see it all. And he seemed to worship her, like a man in love.

She let go of the last frayed threads of resistance, finally believing and trusting him, loving him back.

Now Grace wanted nothing more than to see Mitch as bare as she was. She bracketed his jaw with her hands and planted a deep kiss on his mouth then pulled his shirt up and over his head.

He cooperated fully. Fire flamed in his eyes as he realized she planned to make love to him.

She ran her palms down his chest, loving the feel of his muscles and the light swatch of brown hair along his breastbone, admiring his broad shoulders and strength of him. He was nothing short of gorgeous.

They flew back to kissing like they'd starve if they didn't. Her breasts pressed firmly against his chest, magnifying the heat between them, igniting a fire much deeper inside.

Midkiss she found the drawstring to his scrubs and loosened it, working the thin fabric over his narrow hips, discovering thick muscled thighs and a large bulge in his briefs. His briefs were black, and she liked that, but right now all they did was get in the way. She couldn't wait to tug them down, to see him.

Gone. Finally they were gone, and his full erection felt hard and heavy in her hand. His musky scent made her head spin.

As she explored the smooth skin of his shaft, he cupped her mound, soon discovering how alive and damp she'd become under his attention. Hot and antsy, she squirmed against his palm. A finger dipped inside. She moved against him.

Now her scent mingled with his and nothing would turn them back from sex. She wanted him more than breath and life. They held each other tight and stretched out on the bed. His mouth burned its way down to her stomach while his fingers worked her into frenzy. Soon his mouth replaced his hand, bringing a gentler, deeper touch, driving her wild with long, luxurious pressure. He squeezed her hips, dropping the gentleness and going deep, soon overpowering her. So under his spell, she came quickly and hard, rocking with the energy jetting up her spine and out to her toes.

She gasped her pleasure. "Cooper!" He squeezed her hips tighter, not letting up with his mouth until he'd wrung her to the core.

She thought she'd nearly died, and surely this must be what heaven was like, free-floating over the bed in ecstasy for several long, intense moments.

When he was satisfied she'd completed her orgasm he rose, grabbed her and wrapped her legs around his waist. "I like it when you call me Cooper."

They grinned at each other and crashed onto the mattress with him landing back first, her on top. He smiled proudly, as if he'd just staked a claim, and she belonged to him to do with as he wished. She laughed and shook her head, completely intoxicated by his charm and amazing skills. *Take me, Cooper. I'm yours.*

She shifted her position, wiggled around his erection and clenched the insides of her thighs, rising up to the tip then back down. He groaned. Looked gorgeous doing it, too. "Please tell me you've got condoms."

She went still, wanting to throttle herself. Never in a million years had she ever thought she'd need them in London.

A sexy, though impish expression popped up on his face. "No problem. Hand me my wallet."

Though relieved, she lifted a brow. "For emergencies?" She dug out his wallet from his scrub pocket and handed it to him.

"Been carrying these babies around since the night I met you in the pod." He flashed a victorious grin and handed the first condom to her to do the honors. She laughed again, throaty and natural, marveling at how he always managed to make her lighten up, even now during sex. She couldn't remember ever feeling this relaxed around a man, even before her injuries.

She loved the feel of him as she slid on the condom, firm and throbbing under her touch. She loved the round sponginess of the rest of his assets, too, and stopped to enjoy the full package. He obviously liked that, growing high and tight from her touch.

The deed done, with condom in place she straddled him, guiding him inside while still raw from her orgasm. Immediately she lit up with heat and amazement at having Mitch inside her.

They joined tightly, slowly, easing into each other. She stretched around him, and though she was on top he soon took over the speed and rhythm, bumping up against her, prodding her passion—at this point she needed only minimal prodding.

He moved slowly and gently, then faster and firmer. She leaned her hands on his chest for balance and met every thrust, heat simmering and spreading up to her hips and fanning across her lower back. Frantic to increase the pleasure, she took back control, forcing him deeper, and working him over her most sensitive spots.

Lost in his body and all it offered, she threw her head back and panted with bliss, wanting the thrills to go on and on. His full, steel-like response took her to the edge, held her there suspended in unbelievable passion for what seemed like forever, until she clutched in another orgasm. Eyes tight, shimmering lights behind her lids, matching the fireworks ripping through her body, she collapsed over him.

Catching her, he rolled her onto her back and drove her further and further. His strength grew and forged on. She wrapped her legs tightly around his waist, urging him closer and closer still, feeling his pistonlike passion power on. A groan accompanied a millisecond falter in his pace—"Ahhh, Gracie"—just before he gave it all, pulsating and pumping into her.

They couldn't possibly be any closer than at

this moment—she holding him tight, he resting on her chest, breathing like he'd run a sprint.

Scars were the last thing on her mind.

Only one thought had taken up resident there. Love.

Gracie had fallen hopelessly in love with Cooper.

CHAPTER NINE

THE CELL PHONE blared. Grace rubbed her eyes to help her wake up and checked the clock: 2:00 a.m. A second cell phone buzzed from somewhere nearby, the sound unfamiliar. She reached for her phone. Ethan Hunter's name flashed on the screen.

"Hello?" she said.

"Hello?" Mitch echoed her response after fumbling in the dark for his cell phone, though he whispered.

Surprise gripped Grace for an instant, thinking maybe everything they'd done last night had been a dream. But, no, Mitch was there...in the flesh.

"Grace, this is Ethan." She clicked back into the moment and away from the gorgeous man sharing her bed. She'd had very little interaction with Ethan since she'd arrived, other than the one surgery, and needed time to focus on his early-morning call.

"Oh, uh, yes. Hello, Ethan."

"Sorry for the late call, but I tried to call Mitch and he isn't home. I wanted to let you know that our first Fair Go patient, Telaye Dereje, just arrived from Ethiopia a few hours ago. He's at the Lighthouse."

She heard Mitch talking quietly behind her. "Okay, Roberta. Thanks for letting me know. I'll call him right back."

"Oh, that's wonderful," she replied to Ethan.

"The thing is his injuries are more extensive than we first thought."

Her heart wrenched over the poor ten-year-old child who'd had part of his face blown off in an explosion.

"I've managed to schedule theater time and I'll be joining you and Mitchell there. By the way, I can't reach him. Have you any idea where he might be?"

"Oh." Well, what should she say now? Mitch might not want anyone to know about them. "I'll try to call him as soon as I hang up."

"Thanks. We've scheduled Telaye for seven a.m."

"I'll be there by five. That should give me time to go over his records. We can discuss our approach then. Are you at the hospital now?"

"Yes. Now that I know Telaye is stable, I'm going to take a quick nap. See you soon, then."

"Thanks, Ethan, for pushing this surgery along. I look forward to working with you."

"Same here." He hung up.

She glanced at Mitch, who looked sheepish for a nanosecond before pulling her into his arms for some kissing. "I hear you have a message for me?"

She kissed him back. "Yes, Mr. Cooper." She decided to attempt her fledgling British accent. "You're wanted in Theater at seven."

His devilish smile excited her. "Great. That gives us some time to play."

Their bodies crashed together for some quick, hot, early-morning sex before they napped contentedly in each other's arms for a couple of hours more.

At 4:00 a.m. her alarm went off. She catapulted out of bed and set up the coffeemaker, completely forgetting that she was buck naked. Mitch walked up behind her, wrapped his arms around her waist and pressed her back and bottom firmly against his sturdy wall of muscle, sinew and taut flesh. God, she loved the feel of him. Her head rested back on his shoulder, and he performed an interesting breast examination while they kissed.

One hand traveled downward, over her belly and beyond, pressing and massaging. She felt him lengthen and firm up behind her, prodding between her cheeks. She encouraged him with slow hip rotations. And he was definitely encouraging her.

Forget the coffee, sex would wake them up.

Heated up, she turned round and he lifted her. She bound her legs tightly around his hips as he did an amazing maneuver and wound up inside her.

They'd had a long talk earlier after he'd used the second condom. Their sexual histories were clear and clean as neither had been with anyone in over a year and they'd both been checked for everything with their annual physicals. She was on birth control for no other reason than to regulate her periods, and Mitch knew that, too. Never in her wildest dreams had she thought the Pill might get used for its original reason in London.

With her legs locked around his waist, and him planted inside, he carried her to the bathroom, where she reached out and turned on the hot water in the shower. He utilized those few moments of waiting for the water to warm up by balancing her against the bathroom wall, kissing and thrusting. She never wanted him to stop or to put her down.

Once in the shower he dunked her under the warm water then against the cold tile, but she didn't care. She tipped her hips for better access and, as amazing as the sunrise, they gave each other the best morning gift ever created.

Soon realizing time had gotten away from them, they rushed through the rest of the shower, got dressed and headed for the door. She didn't even bother to dry her hair. Just before Grace could open the door, Mitch stopped her. He looked seriously into her eyes, like a man in love, then kissed her tenderly on the mouth.

"Good morning, Gracie."

She hummed her answer. "Good morning, Cooper." Never having felt so wonderful or alive after so little sleep in her life.

Mitch seemed to know all the shortcuts from her house to the Lighthouse Children's Hospital, just down the road from the Hunter Clinic, and had them in the car park in less than five minutes. Good thing she was staying so close by.

They grabbed some coffee from the doctors' lounge and soon met up with Ethan for a quick meeting at five a.m., exactly on time.

"So here's what we've got," Ethan said, getting right down to business after their early-morning greetings. "Our patient's jawbone, tongue and portions of his face got blown off and it's up to us to repair them."

"I understand we don't have time for harvesting bone and skin from Telaye's leg, like I'd normally do in a case like this," Grace said.

"No," Ethan agreed. "That would require several surgeries and a great deal of healing time in hospital."

"We don't have the luxury of time in Telaye's case," she said.

Ethan nodded his agreement. "Right."

Which meant that Grace's computer-generated models for periodic jaw reconstruction as the boy grew out of one and needed another would go by the wayside.

"What we have is a boy with a severe injury, which requires innovative scientific thinking in order to help." From the sleepless look of Ethan's eyes, Grace guessed he'd spent his night doing research and coming up with a plan. "The boy's deformities also call for us to rebuild what's left of his tongue," Ethan said.

"I was planning on doing that," Grace said, "and to transplant skin from Telaye's thigh to his mouth and jaw."

"Skin, including a vein and artery."

"Absolutely. We have to ensure a solid blood supply for the tissues to encourage regeneration. As soon as we're done here, I'll check which of his legs looks most promising for that."

"Good. You've measured the prosthesis on your computer program?"

She nodded. "It will be a perfect fit for now, and under the circumstances plus room to grow, I guarantee."

"Good." Ethan scratched the short military-style cropped hair on his head. "I've got a wild idea that I think might work due to our time constraints." He looked at Grace, as if testing her mettle. "Have either of you heard about the technique recently performed by two British surgeons on a woman with jaw cancer?"

"The one involving a bicycle chain?" Mitch asked.

"Exactly." Ethan's eyes brightened. "Here's what I plan to do—"

Grace had read about the amazing procedure in a medical journal in the States, impressed with the idea and how it had turned out. So far it had proved successful. This was the kind of out-of-the-box thinking that a field surgeon such as Ethan would come up with for survival's sake, and because he had studied all the latest techniques yet chose this one, she trusted his recommendation.

It could be risky, but Telaye was a growing boy, and a usual jaw replacement would require frequent updates as he grew. It could also be weakened with growth, thus the need for the bicycle chain for added support. Considering where he lived, it simply wasn't feasible for him to have regular surgical updates. This one surgery might be their only chance to help in his lifetime.

"So we all agree to take the risk?" Ethan asked.

Grace nodded. "For Telaye's benefit, yes."

"I'm only the lip man, but count me in, too." After listening intently to the entire conversation, Mitch chimed in and his overwhelming support meant the world to Grace.

Hours later the surgery was going well, but had so far been grueling. Under hot O.R. lights, with perspiration beading on Grace's forehead and upper lip, she inserted the titanium mandibular prosthetic measured perfectly to fit Telaye's jaw, yet still giving him some room to grow.

Next Ethan stepped in and inserted a device

that looked like ordinary bicycle chain made out of titanium to fit around the reconstructed mandible to offer support and flexibility to the newly replaced jaw, and to add the benefit of expanding as the boy grew. Then he attached it with screws to the remaining natural bone.

Grace looked on at his expert surgical technique with fascination. It was as though he'd done this particular procedure hundreds of times.

Every once in a while her gaze drifted toward Mitch, they'd latch onto each other for a brief moment, and though covered by masks, O.R. caps, and splash shields, they still managed to communicate with each other. Her thought was, *I'm so glad I know you.* From the seriously sexy look in his eyes, she suspected he'd quickly done a replay of some of their recent escapades between the sheets, on the kitchen counter and under the shower. The fanciful thought made her grin, and the quick respite from the intense surgery gave her a new wave of energy.

Ethan finished his portion and seven hours into the surgery it was back to Grace to attach the thigh skin, vein and artery—which would take the greatest amount of time—to what was left of the boy's tongue. He might never speak perfectly again, but it would be a lot better than if they left his tongue as it was.

She finished up reconstructing the facial skin flaps over the chin, then turned the last part— lip reconstruction—over to the master, her new guy, the man she loved, "Lips" Cooper.

Utilizing the boy's most recent picture, all carefully measured on the computer screen and set up in the O.R., Mitchell matched the mouth and lips to how the boy used to look. And did another amazing job.

Knowing that their patient was only ten, he'd normally be looking at more reconstructive surgeries as he grew. Under the circumstances, as he lived in a rural village in Ethiopia, they had to make the results potentially last a lifetime. If nothing more, they'd at least bought him several years of looking nearly as good as new, and a damn sight better than when he'd been rolled into surgery.

Truth be told, there was only so much they could

do for Telaye, but all three surgeons agreed he looked fantastic when they'd completed surgery.

Eleven hours later, feet aching all the way up to her hips, Grace ripped off her mask, O.R. cap, gloves and gown, washed up, then collapsed onto a chair in the doctors' lounge. Mitch followed her in, having chosen to be in on the entire procedure, instead of joining the team at his appointed time, and he looked as tired as she felt.

He plopped down next to her and took her hand, aimlessly running his thumb along her knuckles and over her fingers. She mentally cooed, thinking how special it was to have a man supporting and soothing her. Only then did Grace realize she hadn't worn her cover-up. Her arms and scars were on display for anyone who cared to notice.

Ethan walked in, his dark hair spiking out beneath the O.R. cap, observing the couple holding hands and not giving a hint that it mattered to him. Or that he'd noticed her scars. He'd probably seen far, far worse in combat zones.

"Well, that went really well," he said, looking as haggard as she knew she did, though still managing to pull off that handsomely rugged appeal. He shook their hands. Mitch stood to shake his.

"I'm glad you're up on all the latest tricks," Grace said. "Who'd have thought bicycle chain could be the missing link to a stronger mandible replacement?"

"Nice one, Gracie," Mitch said.

She glanced at Mitch and shrugged, not having a clue what he'd meant. Had she said something wrong?

"Bicycle chain? The missing link?" He played imaginary drums on his thighs and hit the nearby table as a makeshift cymbal to accentuate the inadvertent punch line. "We'll have to work on your timing, babe."

"I think you're punchy." She shook her head at his silliness, loving every inch of him, quirky personality and all.

Ethan, on the other hand, pretended not to be amused by the joke, though the corner of his mouth lifted in an almost-smile. He'd quirked a brow when Mitch had referred to Grace as "babe", but didn't comment.

"Well, now that we've got the technique down,

we'll use it for future cases," Ethan said, ignoring the play on words and Mitch's post-op letting off of steam with silly jokes.

"Absolutely," Grace chimed in. "I'm a believer."

He stopped, put hands on his low-slung hips, looking like a man who'd accomplished his mission and now it was time to leave. "Well, then. I'd say take the night off, you've earned it. See you back at the clinic tomorrow."

"Sure thing," she said, noticing it was a quarter past seven.

"See you there." Mitch spoke simultaneously with Grace.

Once Ethan had left, Mitch leaned near and kissed Grace. "Have I told you you're my hero?"

She pulled in her chin. "Your hero?"

"Yeah. You're a natural-born reconstructive surgeon. Gifted as all get-out. I feel honored to know you."

Beaming at his compliment, she kissed him back. "You're not so bad yourself, Lips."

They kissed again. "You know what I miss?" he said.

They'd had sex three times in less than twenty-four hours, and had just come off nearly twelve hours of surgery. How could he possibly—?

"I miss my Mia."

By Grace's calculations, it had been close to twenty-four hours since he'd seen her.

"Why don't you have dinner with us?" he said. "Help me put her to bed. She'd love to see you." He stood, then pulled Grace up by her hands. "All she talks about is when you're coming over again." He smiled brightly at her. "She's going to be thrilled when she finds out about us."

"Isn't it a little too soon to say anything?"

He shook his head. "When a guy meets the one and only woman ever meant for him, he doesn't have to worry about waiting to tell his other best girl in the world. When the timing is right, it's right. When are you going to believe that?"

Taken aback with Mitch's world-tilting words, spoken in such a nonchalant manner, Grace hesitated.

He grew serious again. "I know it's early between us, but besides you being my hero I'm in love with you. I think I have been since the day

I met you in that pod. I just wasn't quite ready for you then."

Relieved that he felt the same way she did, she rushed to his arms. "Mitch, I'm in love with you, too."

"That's a weight off my chest." He smiled and tugged her close, kissed her again. "Thank you."

"For what?"

"For helping me love again."

She savored the sweetest moment in her life, all aches and pains from the long surgery forgotten, just the natural feel of belonging in the arms of the most wonderful man she'd ever met.

"Ditto, Mr. Cooper. Ditto."

"Gracie! Gracie! Read to me!" Mia jumped around in her princess pajamas like a pogo-stick ride gone wildly astray.

It hadn't taken Mitch much effort to convince Grace to have dinner at his house. Roberta had prepared a delicious casserole for dinner, and she was famished. Mia had already had her bath, as she'd eaten hours earlier, and while Mitch and Grace quickly ate the chicken and wild rice with mushrooms and peas, she filled them in on her eventful day.

"What's that?" Mia said, noticing Grace's arms, since she hadn't bothered to cover them up.

"Oh." The observation took her by surprise. "Um, those are my burns."

Mia looked curious, as if she was looking at a bug up close. "Does it hurt?"

"Only at first. I'm okay now."

Without missing a beat, Mia bent down and kissed Grace's arm. "I kissed your hurt. Make it all better."

That was that. Mia had seen her scars, kissed them to make them better and moved on. So matter-of-fact. After Mitch had completely accepted her the way she was last night, and now with Mia doing the same, maybe it was time for her to move on, too.

Grace reached for the child and hugged her tight. She glanced over the child's shoulder at Mitch, who looked on with a somber yet touching expression. "Thank you."

As if a guy could only take so much of squishy good feelings, Mitch got up and started to clear the plates from the table, leaving the girls to do their thing.

After Grace and Mia stopped hugging, and Mia skipped off to her next great adventure, this one having to do with chalk and an easel, she followed Mitch into the kitchen. "Is it okay if I do the bedtime reading tonight?"

"Of course." He stopped making busy work, turning to her. "In fact, I think you should sleep over."

Mia had wandered into the kitchen right at the "sleep over" part and clapped then jumped up and down again. "We're having a sleepover! Yay. Sleep with me!"

Exhaustion and joy mixed together at being wanted by the two most wonderful people in the world, making Grace feel giddy. A laugh bubbled up from her throat. She glanced at Mitch, as he had been the one to bring up the subject of sleeping over. She'd let him tackle this one.

"Uh, Mia…" He got down on one knee, reminding Grace of how he'd done the same for her in her bedroom last night after she'd finally told him the horrible old nightmare. Gushy tender feelings invaded her, seeing him like that again. "I think Grace should stay in the guest room as she's our guest. Don't you?" he said.

Mia gave a full-blown pout for half a second, soon unfolding her arms and smiling, then she clapped again, having instantaneously worked out the solution. She beamed at Grace. "I'll wake you up so we can have breakfast!"

Mitch shot Grace a cautioning look, as if warning it might be the crack of dawn when they'd eat. Happier than she'd been in ages, all she could do was smile. In fact, she couldn't remember smiling this much since before her injuries.

"Okay. I'd like that."

Mitch mouthed, "You'll be sorry," and glanced toward the ceiling.

Mia rushed towards Grace, grabbed her around the thighs and hugged tight. "I love you, Gracie."

How could a kid make up their mind about someone so fast? Well, she and Mitch had made up their minds pretty darned fast. It had been just short of four weeks since she'd arrived in London. She didn't care what level-headed people might think about their whirlwind encounter, she bent over, welling up with precious feelings, and hugged the child around the head then kissed the crown, fresh with children's shampoo scent. "You know what?"

"What?" Mia looked up with those huge and fathomless eyes, just like her father's.

Grace made her own snap decision. "I love you and can't wait to have breakfast with you, either." If she was lucky, maybe it could be for the rest of her life, or until Mia grew up and moved away. Oh, but she'd let her mind travel too far ahead. For now she'd just take it one moment at a time. Besides, savoring each moment was the best way to live. Finally she understood that.

She kissed Mia and an obviously happy and proud Mitch took his daughter's hand and walked her to the bathroom. "Okay, now that that's settled, let's brush those teeth."

Grace had never felt more welcome in her life. She'd never felt she'd belonged anywhere since her accident before this moment either.

Mitch had told her he loved her. She loved him. His daughter loved her. Could life be any more perfect?

She glanced around the living room while Mitch helped Mia with her teeth. The grin that seemed to have been pasted on her face since the moment she'd arrived tonight grew even wider. That picture of Christie was nowhere in sight. She wanted to pump her fist in the air but restrained herself, taking the missing photograph as a very, very good sign.

A few moments later Mitch returned to her and they smiled easily and hugged. "It's your turn. Mia's waiting."

Thinking she'd stepped into a dream, Grace walked down the hall toward a little girl who adored her. She snuggled next to a squirming Mia in her bed and helped her settle down by putting her head in the crook of her arm, near her chest so Mia could hear her heartbeat while she read. The same technique she'd used the other night. She opened Mia's favorite book, the same one they'd read together before, when they'd fallen asleep in each other's arms. *The Tale of Misty Do-Right in the Battle of the Wrongs.*

Fifteen minutes later, with all the Wrongs conquered, Mia was asleep, and the long and difficult day had also caught up with Grace. She turned off the light and walked to the living room, in full yawn.

Mitch was waiting for her. He'd changed into a white T-shirt and bright blue athletic shorts that showcased those great legs. "Everything go okay?"

"Perfect. She's out to the world."

"You look pretty beat yourself."

"And that's not fair because you don't. What's up with that?"

After he gave an affectionate smile, he grew serious. "I know you'll think this is crazy, especially after the way I went after you last night, but I'm actually an old-fashioned guy. Are you okay with sleeping in the guest room?"

A quick, breathy and relieved laugh slipped out. "I'm so exhausted I could sleep anywhere. At this rate I'll be asleep before my head hits the pillow."

He reached for her, held her close and rubbed her back, and it felt so wonderful she thought she might fall asleep in his arms right there in the living room.

"As much as I want to sleep with you, it's for

Mia's sake. I don't want her to be confused when she goes hunting for you bright and early, and you're not in the guest bed."

"I understand. And I think it's a good idea. Though you don't have to put me up here. I can go home."

"No, you can't." He kissed her neck. "I'm too tired to drive you home."

As she often did when in Mitch's company, she gave a light laugh.

"Mia isn't the only one who wants to see you first thing tomorrow morning, you know."

They kissed, and it was hard to pull away from his embrace. But she was beat and was glad she'd brought along her grab-and-go overnight bag, which she always kept at work, knowing she at least had the bare essentials. "Same here."

"In fact, I'd like to see you first thing in the morning for the rest of my life," he said, nuzzling her ear and kissing her jaw.

The statement blasted her heavy eyelids wide open. She pulled her head back and studied him. Unashamed of what had slipped out of his mouth, he smiled benignly.

"I'm just telling it like it is, Gracie."

She put her head on his shoulder and sighed. "I like how you think, Cooper." They swayed in their embrace a few moments, and certain parts of her body started coming back to life, but she was way too tired to do anything about it.

"And who says I can't come and cuddle with you for a while before I hit the sack?" He glanced at her, a hint of devilry in his eyes. "If you want me to, that is."

"I wouldn't have it any other way." The thought of falling asleep in his arms sounded like heaven.

He led her to the guest room by the hand. She followed happily behind.

"I can set the alarm and sneak back to my room before Mia gets up."

"You're a devious genius, Cooper."

The next morning, Mitch and Grace went to the Lighthouse to check on Telaye. The little boy with the bandaged and taped head looked alert and pain-free. Amazing.

"Good morning," Grace said, taking his hand. He couldn't speak but squeezed her hand and she smiled. She glanced at Mitch, who was smiling, too.

She understood the child didn't speak English, and the Lighthouse had brought in a translator.

"How is he this morning?" she asked the young Ethiopian woman.

"He is doing well. No complaints."

"Please tell him we are very happy to hear that."

She spoke to the boy and he looked at them. Grace smiled again.

Leo popped into the room. "Good morning. I've heard from Ethan you did a fantastic job."

"See for yourself," Mitch said.

Grace wondered where Ethan was, but was happy to see Leo in his place. Leo reached for their hands one by one and congratulated them. "You've made headlines today."

"We have?" Grace wondered how word had got out so fast as they all prepared to return together to the Hunter Clinic, a short ten-minute walk from the Lighthouse.

Just as they exited the room Lexi, being the

public-relations maven, showed up dressed to the nines as always, looking ready for her close-up.

"Morning, everyone. Did you see the headlines? I contacted the papers last night, the minute Telaye arrived. Didn't know about that fancy-schmancy new technique you'd used until this morning."

Her huge pink diamond engagement ring never failed to catch Grace's eye. She wondered if her finger ever got tired holding up the ring. Or if she worried someone might try to cut off her finger and run off with the rock.

"Hope you don't mind, but I've scheduled a quick progress report with the press at the front of the hospital in a few minutes. Everyone wants to know about the bicycle chain. Anyone care to talk?"

Grace turned to Mitch with a look of dread. He shook his head. "Not me."

"Me, neither." Grace grimaced, feeling bad, but had to be honest. Facing the press was the last thing she wanted to do this morning. Besides, Ethan was the innovative one; she'd just done what she always did with mandibular prostheses—except for the new bit about rebuilding the tongue. She smiled inwardly with pride.

Having no takers from the surgical team, Lexi glared at Leo. "Leo?"

What could he say? He was the head of the plastic-surgery clinic. She'd put him perfectly on the spot. He flashed a dutiful, though still charming smile. "I'd be happy to, Lexi. Shall we go?"

They left Telaye's room as a group, knowing he was in good hands with the intensive-care Lighthouse nursing staff and the interpreter nearby to explain things to him as they cropped up.

Soon Mitch and Grace said goodbye and splintered off, taking the stairs instead of the elevator. Leo would handle the situation with command and charisma, Grace was sure of it. The only one who could explain the Fair Go charity better would be Ethan, but he was nowhere in sight.

"Aren't Lexi and Iain supposed to get married soon?" Grace asked on the first flight down the stairs.

"I think they're taking off this Friday. They've decided to make it a private affair."

"That's probably a good thing, because Iain

would have to fight off every man with eyes once they saw Lexi's sexy pink dress. Not to mention those six-inch pumps covered in crystals that she's planning to wear."

Mitch turned and gave her a look as if she'd slipped into a foreign language. Yeah, it was a girl thing dressing up for getting married, but such fun!

Grace thought about the silver sequins on the bodice of the pink chiffon dress Lexi had shared pictures of the first night Grace had gone to Drake's with the group. How the sequins started at the shoulders in stripes, worked their way down along the soft and dipping V neck, and gathered at the ribbon waist. How fabulous Lexi had looked when she'd tried it on for the girls at the clinic the day she'd bought it. She had a perfect figure and never flaunted her natural sex appeal. Grace realized she didn't have a drop of envy or insecurity over not having a figure like that. Since making love with Mitch, she'd never felt more womanly and wanted in her life.

"I heard Iain is planning to wear his family

kilt," Mitch said. "Should turn a few women's heads, too."

They laughed, Grace thinking Iain would look fabulous in a kilt, and kind of sorry she wouldn't get to see him.

"Where're they getting married? Maybe I'll crash it just to have a look." She beamed a teasing grin.

"At Marylebone Registry Office, that's what I heard."

The thought of a private wedding sounded fine to Grace. When a person married their meant-to-be love, who cared where they got married? She was sincerely happy for Lexi and Iain.

"Too bad we won't get to see them all decked out," she said.

Mitch squeezed her shoulder. "Oh, if I know Lexi, there'll be pictures, loads of pictures."

She smiled, looking forward to seeing them, as they rounded the landing to the last flight of stairs to the first floor. Warmth flowed through her chest, and it wasn't just from taking the stairs. Life was good.

She loved how spring seemed to be breaking out

at the Hunter Clinic, with Leo and Lizzie leading the way in marriage and now Lexi and Iain. Rafael and Abbie had seemed to have worked through their marital problems, too. And after what Mitch had hinted at last night, she had an incredibly positive outlook for her own future.

When they hit street level and pushed outside, it was sunny and fragrant from the nearby Lighthouse rose garden. They noticed the group of reporters gathered on the hospital entry steps. She smiled and shrugged her shoulders, Mitch did the same, and they turned and snuck off in the other direction, ditching the crowd and leaving the PR up to those best suited for it—Leo and the soon-to-be Mrs. Lexi McKenzie.

Could a day be any more perfect?

CHAPTER TEN

SATURDAY MORNING, MITCH insisted Grace go along with him and Mia for waffles and a special surprise. Even though she had loads of work to make up, she didn't put up a fight—she couldn't think of two people she'd rather spend time with. And since she'd been staying at his house ever since Wednesday, how could she refuse?

It had only been four short weeks since she'd arrived in London, yet a lifetime of troubles had already disappeared. She gazed around and smiled before getting into the car. It was a sparkling sunny day—trees green or in blossom, the air warm and fresh. Even the sidewalks were clean and the drivers polite. As they drove, she rolled down the car window to listen for tweeting birds. Funny how being in love adjusted the attitude that way.

They ate at the same restaurant Mitch had taken

her to for breakfast her very first week in town. But once their orders of waffles arrived, Mitch kept checking his watch. Grace let it slide as she was enjoying the magnificent flavor of blueberries and waffles cooked to perfection.

Later, when Mia dawdled a bit too long over the too-huge-for-one-little-girl fluffy waffle, he encouraged her along. "Eat up, Mia. We don't have all day."

"What has gotten into you this morning?" Grace asked. "I thought you said before we left that we did have all day. Just the three of us, remember?"

"Not exactly," he said, wiping the syrupy corners of Mia's mouth, letting her know she was finished whether she really was or not.

"What's up?" Grace prayed there hadn't been an emergency add-on surgery scheduled that Mitch hadn't told her about.

He sighed. "I want to keep it a secret, if you don't mind."

Surgery? "Well, excuse me," she said, lifting her brows and making a playful, exaggeratedly offended expression. Could this qualify for their first tiff? If so, it was really fun.

He stood. "I'll explain soon enough."

So he was going all dark and mysterious on her. Okay, she could accept that. In fact, he looked pretty sexy that way. Since she liked surprises, she'd go along with his secret plans. Not that she had a choice. Besides, who knew, it might be fun—like just about everything else was with Mitch.

"Where're we going?" Mia had clicked into the conversation. She grabbed one last bite of waffle and shoved it into her mouth.

He checked his watch again. "Too many questions, honeybee." He put a wad of bills on the table, stuffed his wallet back into his pocket and helped Mia out of her chair. "Ladies, just follow me, okay?"

They both opened their mouths to say something. He anticipated it and shushed them before either could make a peep.

Mia looked at Grace and lifted her shoulders, held them by her ears for a second, then burst into a giggle as they dropped. Grace shrugged back.

Mitch was asking her to trust him. Easy-peasy. She'd never trusted anyone more in her life!

"Okay, boss. Whatever you say," Grace said, saluting and taking Mia's hand and following Mitch's wide strides out of the restaurant.

He looked gorgeous as usual, wearing fashionable navy-blue slacks and a designer-brand pink plaid shirt that showed off his flat stomach and broad chest. She loved a man who wasn't afraid to wear pink. He'd rolled up the sleeves. His lightly hair-dusted forearms always struck her as sexy and strong, especially when he unlocked the car door and the sinews flexed ever so subtly.

Yeah, she was in lo-o-o-ve.

They were back in the car and traveling into familiar territory within ten minutes. "Oh, look, Mia, there's the London Eye!" Grace pointed out.

Mia oohed and ahhed, which always put a smile on Grace's face. She loved seeing things through a five-year-old's perspective, as if for the very first time. She smiled again and realized that a smile hadn't left her face in the last three days since she'd been camped out at Cooper's place.

Mitch parked in a nearby lot and they all got out of the car. "I guess I can't keep this a secret any longer. We've got reserved pod tickets for ten-thirty. After all, we are pod people, right? Have to initiate the young adventurer, too. Let's go." To save time, he picked up Mia and they quickly walked toward the ride.

Grace laughed to herself. They were perfectly matched pod people. But Little Miss Adventurer-to-be Mia looked both excited and maybe a little frightened about the four-story-high ride.

"It'll be fun, I promise," Grace said, patting her arm. "I was a little nervous the first time, too."

"Promise?" Mia looked at her with those huge, trusting eyes.

It was never a good idea to fudge the truth to a child, but in this case Grace was perfectly sure. "I promise."

That seemed to do the trick. Mia's little hesitation disappeared, quickly replaced by a wide smile.

There was a separate line for those with reservations, and after a short wait they boarded a pod. Mitch grinned at Grace as if they'd returned to the scene of the crime. He took her hand. Sweet, flirty memories floated through her mind. How he'd seemed so glum at first but soon after she'd struck up a conversation with him he'd switched to charming and fun! How lucky she'd been to get on that particular pod at that particular hour. What if she'd decided not to go that night, or if she'd let her doubts rule the day and had never spoken to him? How different things would have been.

As they started their journey upward, Mia's fears returned and she buried her head in her father's chest. He rubbed her back and hummed. What a great dad he was, and could the man be any more appealing?

She loved him. Without the hint of a doubt. Loved him with all her heart.

"Oh, look over there, Mia," Grace said, attempting to distract her. "That's Big Ben."

Mia peeked up, forgetting how high they were getting, and soon began enjoying the sights along with Mitch and Grace.

About fifteen minutes into the ride Mitch put Mia down and took Grace's hand again. She said a silent thank-you for the man who'd changed her world. His grasp was warm and sturdy, and somehow she knew she could always depend on him.

The pod was crowded and noisy, nothing like the night they'd met, but the magic still snapped between them. They'd staked out a corner with a good view and that was good enough for this girl.

Mitch bent down to Mia. "Remember what we talked about?" She got serious and quiet, as if not quite sure what he really was talking about. He whispered something into her ear, and her eyes went huge with understanding. She made an O shape with her mouth then pinched her lips tightly together, as though she might let out the big secret otherwise.

Thoroughly intrigued and entertained, Grace looked on. So happy to be a part of Mitch and Mia's inner circle, warm, fizzy feelings pulsed through her veins.

Mitch straightened and cleared his throat. "There's something that Mia and I want to ask you."

Now he had her attention full-on. Did he want

her to move in with them since she'd been spending every night there? She could give up her furnished apartment in a heartbeat. "Okay."

At the serious look in his eyes, she went perfectly still, sensing something special was about to happen. The London skyline faded into the background, along with the chatter from everyone in the pod. All she saw and heard were Mitch and Mia. Mitch took one of her hands and Mia took the other one. The hair on her arms prickled with anticipation.

Grace savored this little circle of three with the two most important people in her life: Mitch—the man who'd given her back her self-worth and sensuality, the man who'd shown her complete acceptance, and who'd taught her to love with abandon. And Mia—the child who'd awakened a mother's heart in Grace, then had stolen it.

Mitch nodded at Mia then looked into Grace's eyes. Love and sincerity intertwined in the sexiest eyes she'd ever seen. His lips spread into a tender smile, and he inhaled through his nose as if building courage. "Will you marry us?"

"Yeah, marry us?" Mia slapped a hand over her mouth and covered a delighted squeal.

So moved by the question and rush of full-blown emotion, tears raced to Grace's eyes. She wanted to mimic Mia and clap her hands, but held the wild and crazy feelings in, trying with all her might not to jump up and down.

Being hardly able to breathe and with her head swimming with joy, she answered.

"I'd love to." She looked first into the sparkling sea-green of Mitch's eyes, seeing an ocean of love there. Her hand trembled when Mitch took it, steadying her nerves instantly.

Though it was incredibly hard to tear her gaze away from him, she didn't want to leave Mia out for one more second, so she bent over and pulled Mia close. "I've waited for you all my life." The message could be applied to both of the Cooper clan.

Mia crinkled her nose. "Even before I was born?"

Grace laughed softly and nodded. "Even before you were born I hoped someday to have a child, and here you are."

"Here I am." Mia grinned. "And I get to be a bridesmaid!"

Laughing with unfathomable joy, Grace took both of Mia's hands and squeezed them. "Of course you do."

Mia chattered on and soon got lost in her own thoughts about what her idea of a wedding might be—something that involved swings and slides, ponies and bubbles and...

Mitch took Grace in his arms and high above the Thames and the London skyline he gave her a world-class kiss. Warm, slow, tender and passionate all rolled into one. A kiss of promise. The kind of kiss a guy gave a girl he planned to spend the rest of his life with.

And Grace believed in that kiss and, most importantly, she believed with all her heart in Mitch Cooper.

* * * * *